The nice hands taking the menu drew Vivian to take a closer look at her latest customer.

Beautiful blue eyes that shone bright in a tanned face. Clean-shaven cheeks and chin, which was unusual with the beard phase for the twentysomething crowd. Crisp, overly starched shirt. There was a cowboy hat resting on the table to go along with the open badge of a...Texas Ranger.

"I have nothing to say to you," she said.

"I get it, Miss Watts, and I'm sorry to bug you at work. I'm not here in an official capacity."

"The badge looks pretty official to me."

"Yeah, I get that. I wanted you to know who I am and that I'm legit." He pushed the badge back into his pocket. "I know now's not a good time, but I'd like to ask you a few follow-up questions at your earliest convenience."

"That also sounds very official." She glanced around at the emptying tables. "If you aren't going to order anything, I'd appreciate you leaving. The manager is particular about waitstaff fraternizing with the customers."

"Real order. Real tip. Especially if the tea glass never runs dry." He handed her the menu. "I'm Slate, by the way."

RANGER DEFENDER

USA TODAY Bestselling Author

ANGI MORGAN

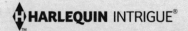

For Shizue, Tamami, Kazuomi and Tosh. Friends whom we miss and love dearly. Thanks for the characters and your years of support!

ISBN-13: 978-1-335-52619-9

Ranger Defender

Copyright © 2018 by Angela Platt

PLEASE RECYCLE

THIS PRODUCT IS RECYCLABLE

Recycling programs for this product may not exist in your area.

Printed in U.S.A.

HARLEQUIN®

™ www.Harlequin.com

Angi Morgan writes about Texans in Texas. A *USA TODAY* and *Publishers Weekly* bestselling author, her books have been finalists for several awards, including the Booksellers' Best Award, *RT Book Reviews* Best Intrigue Series and the Daphne du Maurier. Angi and her husband live in North Texas. They foster Labradors, love to travel, snap pics and fix up their house. Hang out with her on Facebook at Angi Morgan Books. She loves to hear from fans at angimorganauthor.com.

Books by Angi Morgan

Visit the Author Profile page at Harlequin.com.

CAST OF CHARACTERS

Slate Hansom Thompson—A Texas Ranger who wants to defend the innocent, obtaining justice for all. He lives on a ranch with his parents just outside Dallas.

Vivian Watts—A woman who grew up in the system, served her country and majored in international business. She gave it all up to waitress and be near her brother, Victor, who's awaiting trial for murder.

Heath Murray—Lieutenant in the Texas Rangers, Company B, and Slate's coworker and roommate.

Wade Hamilton—Lieutenant in the Texas Rangers, Company B. He has a habit of acting before he thinks things through and always trusts his gut.

Jack MacKinnon, Jr.—Lieutenant in the Texas Rangers, Company B, and Slate's coworker.

Sophia Thompson—Slate's sister. In college, but home on weekends to take care of her laundry.

Therese Ortis—Wade's mysterious friend, who is associated with an unknown organization.

Abby Norman—A sociopath with a very high IQ, multiple neurotic disorders and a desire to achieve the perfect death.

Prologue

From the journal of Dr. Kym Roberts
Case 63047 Evidence Tag 63047-2

Subject Nineteen has been fascinated with death since the patient was thirteen. The subject has not killed squirrels or other small animals. Far from it. The curiosity has led the subject to research what happens at the time of death.

As with many of the subjects in this study, Nineteen is a near perfectionist, becoming more debilitated at every juncture. The patient is so obsessed with the "perfect death," they can't move forward. In some ways this will keep them from the implementation of this fantasy.

The subject is fascinated and refers to "the perfect death" as if something supernatural will occur when it's found. Subject Nineteen stated that begging from the murder victim for their life would not be a necessary part of the "perfect death." Subject Nineteen stated the actual killing would need to be swift and not detract from the scientific approach. The Subject also stated that the death would need to be respectful so dignity is always involved. The planning, the hunt, the capture are all unnecessary details to the perfect kill in their opinion.

Subject Nineteen has described the moment of death to be like a symphony. Each phase building upon itself until there is a crescendo…a wonderful moment of songful bliss. But for the most part, Subject Nineteen can't get past the rehearsal stage. Taking this metaphor one more step, they would not only need the orchestra to perform perfectly, the surroundings would also need to be perfected at the same time.

Only the limits of their perfectionism hold them in check. Wavering from the idea of flawless keeps them from attempting murder. So in Subject Nineteen's case, we hope the obsessive compulsion disorder and need for perfection will prevent the attempt.

Leaving no room for error, the obsessive compulsive need that Subject Nineteen maintains will lead to disappointment and a further downward spiral. This very well may be the source of the night terrors.

Treating one disorder will not resolve the other and possibly will make each worse. And although Subject Nineteen hides it well, the attachment disorder is deeply seated and may be the basis of all the other disorders.

Time is not on our side since eventually, the patient will determine the flaws and overcome. Therefore, Subject Nineteen is a danger to society and should be committed to a facility for a strict psychiatric evaluation and treatment.

EVIDENCE NOTATION

Other entries in this handwritten journal end with a summary of each subject's treatment—if any—along with instructions for other staff members. The treatment summary portion of Subject Nineteen's entry is missing. As in not written or torn from the journal.

Blood spatter pattern indicates the journal was open to Subject Nineteen's page and the deceased was seated at her desk, even though the body was moved to and posed in the chair normally occupied by patients.

A slash from right to left, indicates a left-handed upward movement, which severed the right jugular. Force is consistent with a person standing behind the victim.

Chapter One

"How can a little research and a few interviews get you in trouble?" Wade Hamilton asked. "Besides, I've done all the hard work."

Slate Thompson wasn't on as thin ice as his fellow Texas Ranger. But the entire team knew that one wrong step would shake up Company B—and not in a good way. Wade's hunches about cases were putting more than one of them in the hot seat. So Slate had a right to be wary.

"Then do it yourself," Slate countered.

"You know I'm out of a job if I break ranks again. Come on, you can do this in your sleep, Slate. You're one of the best investigators I know."

"That's beside the point, and if you're attempting to schmooze someone, stating that they *are* the best is better. Especially if it's the truth."

"You read the journal about Subject Nineteen?"

"You stood over my shoulder while I did." Slate stretched backward in his wheeled chair, balancing himself with a booted toe under his desk. He tossed a ball of rubber bands over to Wade. "Moron."

"Just verifying you can read."

Slate popped forward, clicking off the screen as Major Clements walked through the office. Recently, he managed to stop by and check on Wade's progress through the "punishment" boxes—files that were either a last check on cases coming up for trial or completely cold.

"How you doing, Wade? Slate, you aren't busy? Need something to help that along?"

"No, sir. I'm about to head out the door. I...uh...have a lunch date, sir."

Major Clements clapped Wade on the shoulder, then tapped the multiple file folders at the corner of the desk. "Power through, son. We're a little shorthanded out there." Then he continued to his office.

Clements was about fifteen or maybe even twenty years older than either Wade or Slate. But he looked ancient, like a cowboy who had spent one too many years in the saddle. He walked straight, but his belly hung over his belt buckle, a serious silver piece of artwork with the Texas Ranger emblem over the Texas flag. He was one of the few men, in Wade's humble opinion, who wore the uniform's white hat exceptionally well. Like it fit.

Slate, on the other hand, always felt better wearing a ball cap.

"You going to look at that case for me?" Wade whispered. "Victor Watts confessed so it looks like a slam dunk. But my gut's telling me that something's not right. I'd do it myself but..."

Slate waved for him to pass over the file. "You're damn lucky I'm not reporting you to the old man."

"Now, why would you do that, Slate? We get along so well. If I was gone, you'd have to break in another ranger and you know how fun that is." Wade locked his fingers behind his neck and leaned back in his chair.

The bruising had faded, but he was still squinting through a severely beaten eye. The man had spent days in the hospital and come back to work with a cloud hanging around him so thick, everyone was pretending they couldn't see him.

Everyone except Wade's partner, Jack MacKinnon, Heath Murray and himself. They were a team. They'd come into Company B at the same time and had a special bond. Didn't seem like anything could break it.

Even Wade being assigned the punishment boxes.

Most of the reasons Wade had been desked weren't public knowledge. Jack knew more than anyone in the Company and he wasn't talking. But over beers, both Jack and Wade had considered themselves very lucky to have a job.

Jack's temporary assignment to help the Dallas PD hadn't gone without speculation. It also coincided with his new roommate—of the feminine persuasion. Heath, Wade and himself included hadn't spent any serious time with the lady…Megan Harper.

Yet.

Everyone in Company B had seen the results of "the Harper case," as it was referenced. However Wade and Jack had gotten involved, it was Wade's fault for playing a hunch. His saving grace was that whatever he'd done had saved Megan Harper's life and captured a man whose mental health was still waiting to be evaluated.

Saying yes to one of Wade's hunches was usually easy. Hell, this particular ranger had a long line of successful hunches that had played out with many a bad man behind bars. Slate opened the file. He had to admit that he wanted to help.

"You'd be on your own most of the time, buddy," Wade said from the next desk. "Of course, if I'm wrong, then there's nothing to do anyway."

Slate nodded, contemplating. Breaking the rules really wasn't his thing. Then again, he'd wanted to be in law enforcement to help people…not knowingly send an innocent man to jail.

Yeah, there was a chance that Wade was wrong. But when the man went with his gut, he just rarely was.

"I'll do it."

"Why does your intonation hold a giant *but* at the end?"

"Maybe because there is one. I want the story of why you're sitting at this desk instead of on current cases."

"You interview Vivian Watts—Victor's sister—and you'll get it."

"That was easy." But there had to be a catch. The smile on his friend's face was mixed with sadness. Totally not like him.

"Not as easy as you think. Watts's sister moved to Dallas and has been proclaiming his innocence ever since."

"This is a problem because…"

"The trial starts next week. She's going to want to

go public if the Texas Rangers are reopening the case. You're going to have to keep her totally quiet. Still interested?"

"If I say no, you're going straight to Heath with this, aren't you?"

"Yeah." Wade laughed, leaning back in his chair and tossing a pen next to the stack of files.

"He's better with a computer. I'm the best investigator you've ever worked with. Remember?" Slate stood, grabbed the jacket from the back of his chair, shoved his arms through and stuffed his hat on his head for emphasis.

"I think we're remembering that conversation differently. But I'll let you have your exit, Mr. Best Investigator."

Slate left the offices, with Wade's laughter echoing down the hall. He tossed the folder onto the seat of his truck, questioning what he'd just committed himself to. The page of the doctor's notes with the evidence notations he'd read earlier stuck out in his memory:

Other entries in this handwritten journal end with a summary of each subject's treatment—if any— along with instructions for other staff members. The treatment summary portion of Subject Nineteen's entry is missing. As in not written or torn from the journal.

Blood spatter pattern indicates the journal was open to Subject Nineteen's page and the deceased was seated at her desk, even though the body was moved to and posed in the chair normally occupied for sessions.

A slash from right to left, indicates a left-handed upward movement, which severed the right jugular. Force is consistent with a person standing behind the victim.

One case could ruin a ranger's career or come close to it. Just like Wade. Was he willing to risk it? Was he willing to break the rules for someone he didn't know?

Yes.

Hell, did his career actually compare with the lifetime he'd wanted to protect the innocent?

No.

His adrenaline was pumping for once, ready to help someone in need.

Chapter Two

Planning the perfect death wasn't easy, but she wanted one. It was the only way. Abby read the doctor's diagnosis and recommendations every morning. It was in her bedside table drawer, tucked away from the world but in exactly the same place for her daily routine.

She awoke, showered, dressed for her day and read the report as her tea brewed. She might be groggy from a poor night's sleep, but she still put in her contacts and read the torn sheet of notepaper from the journal.

It took her the same number of minutes to read the other papers she'd collected. Three diagnoses over three years from three different cities. Her tea would be ready for a dash of lemon to help her concentrate.

Holistic remedies suited her much better than the prescriptions she'd used since her twenties. Stopping the input of chemicals into her body was the best thing she'd ever done.

It was so freeing.

Her mind could think on multiple levels like it hadn't for the past several years. She sipped the last bit of her tea with her blueberry tea biscuit. More brain energy and antioxidants. She'd need to be on her toes this morning for the next phase of her experiment.

Killing Dr. Roberts had been eye-opening. An epiphany of sorts. Abby no longer was held back by perfectionism. Her death demonstrated it was no longer necessary. The good doctor's analysis had allowed her to move forward last year. Finding the perfect form of death would take practice, yes. But the doctor's death had provided enlightenment—of a sort.

If she couldn't perfect the act of death herself, she'd enlist others to help in her research. Simple enough.

She covered her lips and giggled, ready for her day of research to begin. She couldn't say that she loved this day each week. As Dr. Roberts pointed out, the unfortunate attachment disorder kept her from loving anything. But this day gave her a bit of excitement to look forward to. Moving toward the completion of a project should give a normal person a sense of accomplishment.

And she was so close.

The alarm went off on her phone. She gathered her things from the hall table. Purse, lunch and then the clean surgical gloves and mask from their dispensers. She walked to the door and stood there waiting for it to open, then reminded herself that she had the right to open it when she wanted.

Four years away from the prison they called a hospital and she still had moments where she forgot she was free to move as she wished. It was less than a minute of her life every now and again, but she resented every wasted second it took to force herself to reach out and turn the doorknob.

Thinking about her habits, she crossed the parking lot and climbed the steps to wait under the awning. Dwelling on the idea that her quirks were odd was a waste of time. That's what had sent her to Dr. Roberts to begin with.

A mistake. But a corrected mistake. Using Victor Watts had been an uncontrollable moment of fury. Talking to him before his test had always been nice. Pity because he seemed perfect for the ultimate experiment.

Taking a job at the Veterans Affairs Hospital eighteen months ago had been a moment of brilliance. Her father's attorney had used very little energy to convince the owner of a pathetic little box of a house on Denley Drive to sell. She would have preferred to continue living in the five-star hotel. Her parents could afford it. Instead, her parents insisted things would be better if she didn't.

At least the new house had a specific and organized place designed to meet her more than rational needs. And if she wasn't allowed to drive, walking across the parking lot to the Dallas Area Rapid Transit station was at least convenient. The last time she'd met with her father's attorney, he joked how fitting it was that the two stores nearby were a pharmacy and second-hand shop. He'd laughed at her.

The light rail arrived to take her down Lancaster Road. The job was mundane, her social life nonexistent, but it was all worth it for her research.

The Veterans Affairs Hospital gave her the subjects she needed. Broken, easily manipulated men who had the strength and the wherewithal to perform the necessary duties. *Ha. Duties.* They had the strength to fulfill the experiment Dr. Roberts wrote would never come to fruition.

The doctors were wrong. Everyone was wrong.

Perfection in death was possible.

So close. So so close.

Moving from this venue would be difficult. But working with this group of men and women was coming to an end.

Changing a variable in last week's test would be interesting today. The small amount of excitement she could feel recharged her with purpose.

"Hi, Abby," Dalia said from reception. "Looks like we have a full day of appointments. You're going to be busy."

"Wonderful." She'd practiced the good-morning smile and mimicked the intonation most used when they were excited for their day. The smile that continued on Dalia's face indicated that Abby had managed to keep her voice free of sarcasm.

She picked up the charts as she did every morning and took them to their small, efficient office. There were tapes ready to be transcribed and yes, a full day of veterans checking in for their sleep studies. The private at eight o'clock would be perfect. According to the notes in Simon Evans's chart, he didn't have a history of violence, but she could change that.

She could definitely change that.

Simon arrived right on time. Abby prepped him for his EEG and then the technician applied the nodes to begin the procedure. No one could connect her to the actual study, which was in a sleep lab, on a different floor, on different days. No one at the shorthanded Veterans Hospital ever questioned her competent help.

The electroencephalogram monitored brain waves while a patient slept. It set up a baseline and then monitored the volunteers throughout the sleep studies. Perfect for her needs since each participant needed a session per month.

Two of her experiments had succeeded recently.

It wouldn't be long. Not long at all.

Simon was snoring. She checked the monitor. He seemed to be in full REM. She locked the outside door so they wouldn't be disturbed, cautiously placed earphones over Simon's head and turned on her carefully recorded message.

For the next hour, her softly spoken words about injustice, violence and murder repeated. Keywords that helped the subject draw the logical conclusion that death was the only possible solution for their problems.

The tape ended. Three hours of sleep was all the patient was allowed. The timer dinged, she awoke Simon and alerted the technician it was time to finish. Once he cleaned up, she brought the questionnaire to be completed along with the second page for her own study.

Simon passed the next appointment on the way out— Private Second Class Rashad Parker with debilitating night terrors. He'd already tried to choke his girlfriend in his sleep. Abby went through all the steps, waited until he entered rapid eye movement and introduced her tape.

Curiosity was the closest she got to elation. She

thought Rashad would have succumbed to her mind-manipulation last week. With her new keywords, culmination was probable within the next couple of days.

Wouldn't Dr. Roberts be surprised if she was still around?

She covered her lips and giggled.

Chapter Three

Wiping down yet another table, Vivian Watts stepped back to let a man slide into the booth. "I'll be right back with a menu."

The lunch rush was over and in another hour she'd be off until she came back for the double tomorrow. And then she'd be done and never wanted to see another chicken wing as long as she lived. When she told the manager she'd need off next week for the trial, he agreed and promptly fired her.

Nothing personal, he'd said. Of course it was, she'd replied. And that was the end of the conversation. One more day to feel greasy. At least she'd be clean while standing on the precipice of bankruptcy.

Was it really bankruptcy if you didn't own anything to be lost? Probably not. So technically, she'd be homeless without two shiny dimes to her name. Technically.

If all else failed, she could reenlist in the army. Who knows, this time she might be a commissioned officer since she'd earned her degree. She really didn't want to go back into uniform. Of course, it would be better than wearing this little chicken wing thing.

She dropped the dirty stuff behind the bar, stuffed her last tip into her apron, grabbed a water and snatched a menu on her way back to the new table. It would be another single instead of the four-top that just filled up.

"Here you go. Can I get you something else to drink?" The nice hands taking the menu drew her to take a closer look at her latest customer.

Beautiful blue eyes shone bright in a tanned face. Very clean-shaven cheeks and chin, which was unusual with the beard fad for the twentysomething crowd. Crisp, overly starched shirt. There was a cowboy hat resting on the table to go along with the open badge of a…Texas Ranger.

Open in the way they identified themselves. "I have nothing to say to you."

"I get it, Miss Watts, and I'm sorry to bug you at work. I'm not here in an official capacity."

"The badge looks pretty official to me."

"Yeah, I get that. I wanted you to know who I am and that I'm legit." He pushed the badge back into his pocket. "I know now's not a good time, but I'd like to ask you a few follow-up questions at your earliest convenience."

"That also sounds very official." She glanced around at the emptying tables. "If you aren't going to order anything, I'd appreciate you leaving. The manager is particular about wait staff fraternizing with the customers. He particularly hates it."

"Oh, I'm ordering. I'm starved. I'd like a basket of ranch habanero wings, side salad, fries and sweet tea."

"This is a real order. You're not expecting it on the

house or anything? If you want the cop discount, I have to get the manager or it comes out of my check."

"Real order. Real tip. Especially if the tea glass never runs dry." He handed her the menu. "I'm Slate, by the way."

"I'll be right back with your tea."

A week before Victor's trial and a Texas Ranger shows up saying it's unofficial business? Hope. A slim chance of it bubbled into her heart. Just as quickly, her rational mind took out a needle and popped it.

It had been over a year with no hope. A year of visiting her brother and faking a positive attitude so he didn't lose all hope. She wouldn't allow this one man who was here in an unofficial capacity to rattle her heart.

All the emotional strength she had left was reserved for her brother. Period.

Tea and salad to the table. Menus to another. Sneak a look at the ranger who's watching something on his phone. Clear and wipe down a booth. Salt shakers filled for the next shift. Order up. Wings for the ranger.

"Need anything else?" she asked, sliding the basket in front of him.

He performed an ordinary shake of his head just like many customers had before him.

"Why should I talk to you without Victor's lawyer present? Not like he'd know what to do if I wrote it all out for him. Why should I listen to you?"

"I just have a question."

"For me?" She stuck her thumb in her chest, realizing too late that it drew his eyes to the bulging cleavage her waitress outfit emphasized. "Not Victor?"

The ranger dropped his hands in his lap and looked at her. Really looked at her, like very few people had in the past year.

"I can't make any promises, Vivian. I just picked up your brother's file this morning, but I have a question that I hope you can answer. Maybe it'll lead to another question. That's all I've got at the moment."

Honesty. Clarity.

And a trickle of hope.

"I...uh...I get off at two." She was about to cry because of that one snippet of misplaced emotion.

"Can I meet you—"

"I no longer own a car, officer."

"Slate's fine. There's a coffee shop three doors down. That okay?"

"Sure. I'll get your check."

She turned quickly and used the corner of the bar towel to wipe the moisture from her face. Maybe he hadn't seen it. Who was she trying to fool? Looking at her—really looking and connecting with her eyes—that's *why* she was crying.

He'd seen it.

She punched in his ticket number and waited for the printout. No one else noticed her shaking hands or her racing heart. No one noticed anything except her hurrying through the rest of her shift.

Slate finished his wings with half a pitcher of tea still on his table. She'd dropped it off so he wouldn't run out. He paid and was gone forty-five minutes before she finished up.

She grabbed her jacket and wished she'd brought a change of clothes. Having a serious, even unofficial conversation in the short, revealing T-shirt would be hard. She could keep her jacket on.

Sure. Coffee. That's all this was. One Frappuccino and one question.

With the stupid hope that it would be another…and then another…

And then the reopening of her brother's investigation and surely proving that he was innocent. No trial. They could go home.

Oh, my gosh. That was why she hadn't let herself hope during the past year. One small peek at the possibility and she was back to leading a normal life in Florida. She couldn't do this to herself and certainly couldn't do it to her brother.

She hated…hope.

Chapter Four

Meeting Vivian Watts at work seemed like a smart thing to do, until Slate remembered the waitress uniforms at the restaurant. But that was after he'd walked through the door and asked for her section. Immediately noticing how smoking hot she was stopped coherent thought.

And then she'd cried.

Mercy. He was just like any man wanting to do the right thing. He wanted her to stop crying.

He knew he could help make that happen. All he had to do was find a murderer.

Choosing a table in the far back corner of the coffee shop, he opened a file no one in the room should see. The chicken wings sat like a lump in his gut. Maybe the acid from the strong brew would help with the digestion. Good thing he didn't have a weak stomach or he'd be losing it all by studying the murder scene pictures.

He wanted to help Vivian and Victor Watts. But it did all boil down to one question that no one had ever asked her brother.

"Officer."

He flipped the file shut and stood, pushing back his chair. "You want something?"

"No. I'm fine." Vivian sat and pulled her coat tighter.

It was sweltering hot inside the shop despite the November chill that hung outside. Well, she was wearing hot pants and half a T-shirt.

"It's Slate. Lieutenant if this was official, but again, I can't make any promises."

"I stopped believing in promises about the time my brother was arrested for murder. Every promise that was made to us by the Dallas police was broken. And then there's been the three court-appointed attorneys who *promised* they'd find the real murderer."

"I'm sorry you've had to go through this experience. It doesn't feel fair, but the evidence does point to your brother."

"Spare me, Lieutenant. Until you've lost everything you've had and are about to see your only family convicted of murder in a state that has the death penalty... Please, just ask your question so I can go home."

"Sure." He opened the file to a copy of the murder victim's journal entry. "Can you tell me if your brother ever participated in a study performed by Dr. Roberts?"

"The answer is already in your file. He was seeing her for a sleep disorder. Night terrors. Yes, he knew the victim. Yes, he had an appointment with her the day she was murdered. No, he'd never mentioned that he had a problem to me. No, he never mentioned wanting to kill anyone. No, he hasn't been the same since he was discharged from the army." She pushed away from the table. "Thank you for taking a look at Victor's case. But I really have to get home—"

"Subject Nineteen. Was that your brother's number?"

"What are you talking about?" She sank back onto the metal chair.

"No one's ever mentioned how your brother was linked to the murder before?"

"All I know is that my brother was participating in a VA-approved sleep study sponsored by Dr. Kym Roberts. She was one of the doctors conducting the study where she was murdered."

"That's all in the file."

"So what does this subject number mean?" It was actually the answer he wanted to hear.

Watts was a part of the study. The police had verified that much. But there was nothing in the file verifying he was Subject Nineteen. What if it was a different person? They'd have another suspect. But he couldn't share something like that. It would wreck the prosecution's case. Slate wouldn't get "box" duty like Wade. He'd be looking not only for a different job, but a different profession.

No one would hire him if he shared that type of information.

"I can't show you the evidence."

"You mean whatever made you question Victor's innocence?"

"Yes. So you've never heard of his status in the study as a subject number?"

"As far as I can tell, it wasn't a blind study if that's what you're referring to. I have a copy of it at home.

It doesn't include the names of the participants but it has information specifically for Victor. Do you need it? Could I bring it to your office tomorrow?" Vivian scrunched her nose, sort of grimacing.

"You said you don't have a car. Perhaps I could give you a lift home."

"There's an office supply store around the corner from my apartment if you need copies."

"That'll work."

"Lieutenant, I know you said you weren't reopening Victor's case. It does sort of sound like you've found something new." She bit her lip, pulling her jacket even tighter around her.

"Why don't you show me the copy of the report you have? That's the first step."

The sky broke open in a severe thunderstorm that had been threatening all day. Slate stuck his hat on tight, tucked the file into his shirt and gestured for Vivian to stay at the door. "No sense in the both of us getting soaked. I'll be right back."

Slate ran the two blocks to his truck, dumped his hat in the back seat, locked the file in the middle compartment and drove back to the coffee shop. A little over ten minutes. But when he pulled up outside, Vivian wasn't standing near the door. He waited a couple more minutes. Then he pushed on the flashers and ran inside to see.

"Hey." He got the attention of the barista. "Where's the woman I was with a few minutes ago?"

"You left. She left. I don't know where."

"Well, if that don't beat all."

Cranking the heat once inside the truck, he dialed Wade.

"So?" his friend asked first thing.

"I met with her. How 'bout you look at the list of things in the evidence file?" Slate paused, slapping the file against his thigh waiting while Wade pulled up the rest of the information.

Information he'd deliberately left out to entice Slate to look further into the case.

"Got it."

"Is there a follow-up report from a sleep study that the victim was conducting?"

"Nothing."

"So if I thought the list was necessary to answer the questions that we had…"

"I knew it!" Wade said with force, then repeated himself in a lower voice. "You'd need to sweet-talk a copy, not request it through a warrant. Seriously, Slate, if you have those kinds of doubts, take it to the district attorney's office."

"I need a couple more things clarified and then I'll head there."

Yeah. A couple more questions like…why didn't Vivian wait at the coffee shop? He opened the incomplete file Wade had given to him to pique his interest, then added Vivian's address to his GPS. Traffic was pretty bad in the downpour. He wasn't surprised that someone who didn't own a vehicle lived right on the bus route, but he was surprised that Vivian wasn't home.

He was already soaked but standing on an apartment doorstep would only draw attention to himself. And it was getting colder by the minute. So he waited in the truck. He had a perfect view of the door, but several minutes later, there was a knock on his window, followed with a gesture to roll it down.

"Get in!" he shouted.

Vivian ran around to the opposite side and jumped in the front seat. Soaked to the skin, still dressed in the short shorts and T-shirt.

"I thought we agreed I'd give you a ride."

"I appreciate it, Lieutenant, but I didn't want there to be any misunderstandings." She dripped on the papers she had in a folder. "The top copy is the original. You can see that the cover letter is a diagnosis and the results of the study."

"They mailed this to you?"

It didn't look identical to the other report even though it began the same.

"To my brother. This is where he lived prior to his arrest." She opened the door. "I'll be heading inside now. Thanks for looking at Victor's case…even unofficially."

"But I'm not."

Too late. The door was shut and she ran up the sidewalk. So he took the time to compare the two papers.

This report was in the same tone as the journal page. Formal, doctorly, professional. And dated recently. It was also signed by an assistant who had been interviewed just after the doctor's murder. The statement, along with numerous others from hospital staff, was in the file. The recent report…was not.

Nothing new.

Except there were names. Summaries of group sessions. No one was referred to as a subject and there sure
as hell wasn't a Subject Nineteen.

"Damn. They have the wrong guy."

Chapter Five

"Your brother's innocent."

"I know."

Vivian opened the door wider, no longer embarrassed that the one-room furnished apartment had a pullout couch and a kitchenette with half a refrigerator. She'd passed that stigma three months ago when she calculated she'd be out of money by the beginning of the month.

One more week before the trial and two more days with a roof over her head.

She gestured for the Texas Ranger to enter and wait on the cracked linoleum by the door. "Let me get you a towel."

On the way to the bathroom, she shoved the bed into its couch position and tossed the cushions back on it. But another glance at the ranger confirmed that he was soaked to the skin...just like she'd been a couple of minutes earlier.

"There's a fold-up chair behind you."

"That's okay, I don't mind standing. And dripping." He laughed.

Lieutenant Slate had a good laugh. Deep and sincere that crinkled the skin near the corner of his eyes. She pulled a clean towel from the shelf and caught herself checking what she looked like in the mirror. And then picking up the hand towel and wiping the nonwaterproof mascara from under her eyes.

She tossed the towel across the small area into the ranger's hands. He took off his hat, looking for a place to set it, then carefully flipped it upside down into her— thankfully—empty sink.

Briskly, he brushed the worn cotton across his short hair, then used his hand to slick it back down again. "Sorry about the puddle."

"No problem." She sat on the couch, tucking her cold feet under her, seriously glad that she'd put on lounge pants instead of jumping into the shower.

"You're very patient," he said, shifting his boots into a wider stance. "If someone told me my brother was innocent after he'd confessed to a murder, I'd be chomping at the bit for an explanation."

"I'm tired, Lieutenant Slate. That's all. And you'll have to forgive me for not being excited about your announcement that you are not reopening his case. I've known my brother was innocent from day one."

"It's just Slate, ma'am. Slate Thompson. And I get it."

"And I'm Vivian. Definitely not a ma'am." She gestured to the end of the couch. "Please sit. A little water isn't the worst thing that's been on that cushion."

"If you're sure?" he asked, but he was already shrugging out of his jacket and hanging it over hers on the back of the door.

When he turned around, she saw the file folder with the sleep-study report stuffed into the back of his jeans.

"That was one way to keep it dry."

"Yeah." He pulled it around front and tapped his palm with it several times. "So, this report sheds a new light on your brother."

"I'm not a silly, inexperienced sister, Lieutenant Thompson." By using his formal name, she wanted to keep things a little more professional than they looked in her shabby studio apartment. "Honestly, I turned over the original report to Victor's attorney the day after it arrived here. He said there was nothing he could do with it. That it didn't prove anything since the prosecution had already submitted the study as proof of his guilt."

The momentary elation she'd felt in the coffee shop had long passed.

"I disagree." He leaned forward, resting an elbow on his thigh in order to look at her and handle the copy at the same time. "This isn't the report that's in the file."

Had she heard him correctly? "I'm not following."

"This report was written by Dr. Roberts's assistant and sent to the participants nine months after Victor's arrest."

"So it couldn't be a major part of the prosecutor's case, right? I'm so stupid."

"I wouldn't say that."

"How could I have missed something that evident?"

"Look, Vivian, don't beat yourself up. You don't have access to the evidence. I wouldn't either if it hadn't been a ranger who made the arrest."

She sat forward, close enough on the small couch that

Slate's heat rose like steam around him. There was no use trying to keep the relationship professional. He'd be a family friend for life when they got her brother out of jail.

"So what happens now? Do you need Victor's lawyer or do you have all that information in the file? I should get dressed. I want to be there when you tell him." She stood and realized he hadn't moved.

He dropped his head and tapped the papers onto his palm again.

"What? I thought you said this would clear him?" She crossed her arms and wanted to look angry, but was afraid she looked a little ridiculous in her silky lounge pants and sweatshirt. Tapping her bare toe on the old carpet didn't present too much power either.

His hesitation only made her angrier and more anxious.

"Mr. Thompson, please." She let her arms drop to her sides, afraid the tears would return and she'd totally lose it this time. "Just tell me."

"I'm not supposed to be here." He finally made eye contact with her. "I work for the other side. You get that, right?"

"And you'd want to sentence my brother to death even knowing he's innocent?"

"No. That's not it." He jumped to his feet.

The small room had never seemed as small as at that very moment. It wasn't that Slate towered over her. She wasn't a short woman, but the panic she'd been warding off consumed her. It covered her like a suffocating blanket and she had a hard time breathing.

The more air she took in, the less she could breathe.

"Vivian, look at me. I'm not going to hurt you."

His hand covered her mouth. She dug her fingernails into the side of his hand attempting to remove it. It wouldn't budge. She felt the panic of not being able to breathe but forced a small amount of air through her nose.

"Listen to my voice. You're hyperventilating, Vivian. I'm going to help you slow down your respirations. Try to count backward from ten in your head."

He tugged her one direction and went the other. Ending the move so they faced each other. "That's it. Deeply through your nose."

She shook her head, feeling the panic again with the lack of oxygen. *Ten.*

"In."

She sniffed as best as she could.

"Now let it out."

The sound of her breath hitting his fingers was weird.

"In."

It was broken, but she managed, catching the hint of coffee on him. *Nine.*

"Deeper," he whispered closer to her ear. "Let it out slowly."

She obeyed. *Eight.*

"You got this. Now I'm going to take my hand away. Just keep breathing in and out."

Freedom washed over her as he dropped his hand and took a step away.

"In. Out. Just think calm."

Seven. She covered her face, unable to look into his obviously concerned eyes.

"You okay now?"

"I think I can... That's...that's never happened to me before."

"I apologize for the up close and personal, but I didn't have a paper bag in my pocket."

She swayed and his hands darted out to steady her. "Whoa. I think I'm a little light-headed."

"No surprise. Why don't you sit again? I'll get you a bottle of water." He helped until the back of her knees bent against the couch and she sat.

"Tap. Glasses..." She pointed above the sink. The dishes were on an open shelf. He wouldn't have trouble finding them. "That was...so embarrassing."

Slate moved his hat out of the sink and filled a glass, then handed her the water. "Do the panic attacks happen often?"

"Never."

He looked at her like that was hard to believe, but he didn't say the words. "I figure this is a lot to take in. You're gonna have to trust me."

"Does that slow-talkin' cowboy act work on a lot of the girls?" She watched his puzzled reaction. Had she miscalculated him? Was he for real? "Look. I don't trust anyone anymore. Victor and I have been screwed over by the best of them. Just tell me what's wrong with this report and why aren't we on our way to the attorney's office?"

"Yeah, about that." He grimaced slightly while sucking air through his teeth. Then he arched his hand down the back of his head and scratched his neck. Then he put his hands in the air like he was stopping her from moving. "You're not going to have another attack, are you?"

She crossed her arms and legs in answer.

"My buddy was checking the file to make sure everything on our end is ready to go next week. Heath might have arrested your brother, but no one in my Company had anything to do with the investigation."

"So?"

"I don't actually have permission to be working the case."

"Oh. I understand. You'd rather not be involved so you're going to let my brother hang."

"No, that's not exactly what I meant." He pulled his phone from his back pocket.

"Mr. Thompson, it's time for you to leave." She stood and pointed to the door.

He held a finger up in the air with one hand, bringing his phone up with the other. "One second. Just give me—Wade. Look, your hunch was right. Yeah, I've got a good lead, but I'm going to need some time. No." He brought his light blue eyes up from looking at the carpet to meet hers. "I did not get food poisoning. I'll put in for the time off. I just wanted to be sure you'd be around for tech support. Yeah, man. *One* of the best." He disconnected, shaking his head then rubbing his forehead right between his brows.

"What was that about?" she asked, trying not to feel pleased or excited or both.

"I'm going to help you." He took off his badge

hooked on his shirt pocket and tucked it away with his ID. "I just can't be a Texas Ranger while I do."

"You're really going to help me? Help Victor?" That bubble was back, ready to pop with his next words.

"I didn't sign up for this job just to step aside and see an innocent man go to prison." He stepped back toward the kitchen and picked up his hat, now on the two-burner stove. "Now that you know the logistics on my end, let's go see Victor's attorney. I'll be in the truck while you dress. It's still raining out there. You might want to bring an umbrella."

Was that a wink while he secured that Stetson on his head?

It didn't matter. She felt years older than Slate Thompson. And her heart was a little short on...

Well, everything. It was depleted. Empty. Desperate for any human kindness.

The tears came as soon as Slate pulled the door shut behind him. Just a short, easily controlled attack while she gathered clothes.

Who knew what they'd be doing later. And she meant *they*. There wasn't any way in the world she was letting that cowboy get out of her sight until she found out everything he knew about Victor's case.

Slate had only met the poor, pitiful, chicken wing waitress in dire need of help. He had no idea what she became when she put on her business suit. It might be her last one, but she looked and felt like she was in control.

Normal.

Chapter Six

Half an hour passed. Then another ten minutes. Slate was stepping out of the truck to see what was keeping Vivian when her apartment door opened.

It was one of those jaw-dropping moments that didn't happen very often in his life. He'd kept it together and hadn't cracked a smile in his Department of Public Safety days when a girl took off her top trying to get out of a speeding ticket. The man who thought his clothes were on fire and spit a bottle of water all over his uniform—he'd handled it all with a straight face and no disgust.

But seeing Vivian Watts step onto the wet sidewalk in a blue suit made him take a second look. And maybe a third. Her wild dark brown hair was neatly tucked at the back of her head. He noticed because he ran to her side of the truck and grabbed the umbrella she'd brought with her.

Helping her onto the front seat, he politely waited for her to put down a towel. It gave him plenty of time to admire the line of her calf and the height of the matching blue heels. Not to mention a close-up view of the shapely behind in her tight-fitting skirt.

The wolf in him came out. His lips were all puckered to let loose a howling whistle when he caught himself and kind of sucked air through his teeth. She noticed. Yep, she smiled, knowing what was blowing through his mind.

He ran to his side of the truck, chucking the umbrella in the back seat. His tie had been off since he'd left for lunch, but the way she was dressed almost made him feel guilty enough to put it back on.

Almost.

"I'm assuming we need to go to your place for you to get dry clothes. I'm fine with that by the way."

"I live west of the metroplex on a ranch. It's sort of out of the way."

"So the cowboy thing isn't a thing? It's genuine?"

"That'd be me."

"You don't mind being wet?"

"Well, I've been worse. Beer once. Now that's sticky when it dries." Slate had already looked up the address of the attorney in Uptown.

"As much as I'd like to hear about you covered in beer… I think you take a left here."

"Not around this time of day. It really is a funny story."

"I gather."

Slate tapped on the radio, immediately turning it down. "You don't have to worry. I looked at directions and traffic before you got in the truck."

"Do you think we should talk about what happens

now? How do we get the report if Victor's attorney didn't keep the copy I gave him? Are you sure you know how to get to his office? I think you missed another turn."

Lots of questions he wasn't prepared to answer. "Let's just take it one thing at a time. First step is to get there and ask for a copy of the study. We compare. We might get lucky."

"Lucky? How long have you been a ranger?"

"Almost two years. I was fortunate to be stationed here in Garland. That's close enough to help out my family. How about you? What did you do before you came to Dallas or have you been here awhile?"

"I studied international business and had an internship at one of the top companies in Miami."

"You gave all that up to come help your brother."

"That didn't sound like a question."

Slate stated fact. He admired her for it. She didn't know there was a personal financial report in the file. One reflecting she and her brother were broke. He'd read her statement to the police, an interview that confirmed most of the information obtained through the VA.

"Are you going to tell Victor's attorney that you're reopening his case?"

"One step at a time, remember?" Slate didn't have permission to do anything. Unfortunately, the attorney would know that. "Why don't you tell me about your brother?"

"As in…?"

"What problem was he having? Something like he couldn't sleep, right?"

"Night terrors. He's had them since returning from the Middle East. He's never really talked to me about his time in the army. The most common question from you guys is do I think he's capable of killing someone." She paused, taking a look out the window. "The answer is I don't know. I haven't spent a lot of time with him after he left the military. He came to Dallas because of Dr. Roberts and her study. He wanted to be a part of it and live a normal life."

"Look, Vivian." He was about to cover her hand but he redirected his hand to the steering wheel. "I'm on your side. Honestly, I don't know if they'll reopen the investigation. I'm pretty sure the prosecutor will fight it since he thinks his case is pretty solid."

"Then what are we doing?"

The windshield wipers banged out a rhythm, adding a slow swish as the rain turned to a sprinkle. "Not giving up."

"I never did."

He turned to face her, seat belt stretched tight across his chest. "If your brother is truly innocent…neither will I."

Where the hell had that come from? That whole fighting-for-justice thought earlier? Maybe. More than likely. It couldn't have anything to do with the wolf whistle he'd swallowed along with the urgent need to puff up his chest and rescue the fair maiden. Naw… nothing like that.

Or exactly that.

He'd wanted to help Vivian and her brother since meeting her in that ridiculous waitress outfit. The suit, however, fit her to perfection. It was much sexier than the skimpy shorts. Even though he'd enjoyed looking at her legs.

Someone behind him honked a horn. The light was green and he continued to the law office. He parked and Vivian didn't open her door.

"Look, Slate. As much as I appreciate your promise, I'm not holding you to it. You seem like a nice guy. I have no idea why this is happening to my brother, but it's not your responsibility."

"Let's talk to your lawyer and compare the reports. See what he thinks is going on. Throw around some ideas. Then maybe we can grab dinner and talk."

VIVIAN WAS RELUCTANT to walk down the street with Slate to one of his favorite restaurants. The visit with Victor's lawyer had been a bust. Even her favorite suit couldn't make her feel better about the cavalier attitude he'd shown by not keeping the appointment.

It began to sprinkle again. Slate grabbed her hand and hurried through the dinner crowd on Maple Avenue and crossed the street.

"Here we go. I'm starved." He released her hand and shot both of his through his hair, slicking the longer portion on top straight back like he had in her apartment.

"You just ate three hours ago." She swiped droplets of water from her sleeves, then pulled a curl back under control, tucking it behind her ear. "Slate, I…um…I can't eat here."

Sam and Nick's was the third most expensive steak house in Dallas. She knew only because she listened to customers talk about the amazing places they'd been to—other than her chicken restaurant. She had agreed to come with him to dinner, but she wasn't going to order anything. She couldn't. The money in her wallet was bus fare to get her back and forth to court.

"Sorry, I should have asked if you're a vegetarian or vegan. Look, there's a place every fifty feet around here. I'm sure we can find one for non-meat eaters." He grabbed her hand again.

The doorman stared at them.

"I'm not a vegetarian," she whispered. Then she leaned in closer to him. "This place is too fancy for me."

"Well, shoot. My mouth is salivating for a good sirloin." He took a step away from the door, letting another couple pass through. "Wait. This is my idea. My treat. Can we eat here now?"

As much as she'd lowered her voice to avoid embarrassing looks, Slate spoke loudly, not seeming to catch a hint of her embarrassment—at all. He tugged gently on her hand, backing up to and through the open doorway.

The maître d' recognized Slate as he turned around to face her. "We can seat you right away, Lieutenant Thompson."

The couple that was before them had just been told it was a forty-five minute wait. Vivian looked at the ranger and he promptly winked at her. He also still had hold of her hand. Firm grip.

"They do have really good sirloin here."

"So this really is one of your favorite places. They know you on sight."

He bent close to her ear, his warm breath cascading over the sensitive lobe. "I sort of stopped a robbery one night. They won't let me forget it." He jerked his chin to a framed article hanging on the wall.

Well, how about that. He was a real-life hero. She got closer, along with the couple now behind them in line, and read all about the armed robber who hadn't made it out the door because a Texas Ranger had been dining here.

"Thank God. That's the first gun we've seen out in the open like this," the woman in line said. "I didn't know what to think. Do you wear your weapon when you're on a date?"

"Actually, ma'am—" Slate's accent turned super slow and drawn out "—I'm required to have it with me at all times. Unless I've been drinking, of course."

The maître d' returned and Slate's heavily countrified accent disappeared as he spoke with Candace—he knew the young woman by name—and asked her how her son was getting along at his new daycare.

Seated at a table for two near the corner, Slate held out Vivian's chair and seated himself against the wall. He waved off the menus.

"Mind if I order for you?"

"Not at all." She might as well let him. If he was buying, she wouldn't have to look at the prices and wonder how she'd ever repay him.

"Double the usual, Mikey. And how's your kid brother? He going to pass chemistry?"

"Yes, sir, Senor Slate. We got him the tutor and it was free. Just like you think." The waiter raised his brows and looked at her. "You want a drink, Miss? And house salad dressing like Senor Slate?"

"That would be great, and water's fine. Thanks."

"He's a good kid," Slate said as Mikey walked away. "When his father was killed, he had to quit high school to support his family, but he got his GED."

She was almost speechless. Almost. "Are you for real? I mean, I thought there was some reason you were offering to help me. Some gimmick. Or something that you're hiding from the police. But it seems like you genuinely care. Do you?"

Slate Thompson looked surprised. No, he actually looked terrified.

"I hadn't… I…"

"Don't worry, Slate. Your secret's safe with me."

There weren't too many people in the world who truly cared about others anymore.

"I'm sorry we didn't have a chance to discuss the case with your— I need to take this." He withdrew his phone and answered. "What's up? No, I'm in Uptown. Yeah, twenty minutes with sirens. You're certain? I'll check it out."

"Don't worry about me," Vivian said, "I'll take the bus home."

"There's been a murder-suicide at the VA Hospital. One of the men in the same study as your brother." He scanned his phone. "If you don't mind waiting in the truck, I can take you home after. Easier than trying to find the buses in the rain. Come on."

He asked the waiter to make it a to-go order, paid the bill and left her to go get his truck.

"He's such a nice man," the maître d' said after the door shut behind him. "He saved my life during that robbery. The guy held a gun under my chin and said he was going to blow my head off. After the whole terrifying thing was over, Slate brought a counselor by to talk with me before my shift a couple of days later. There's no way I'll ever be able to repay him."

"He seems very kind." *Amazing is more like it.*

"Here's your order," the waiter said, handing her the bag of food.

Right on cue, Slate pulled up under the awning.

She climbed into the passenger side. "I don't want to be a bother, Slate. You could drop me at the Rapid Transit station and I can get home from there."

"You'd ruin your shoes waiting in the rain. I promise, I won't be long. Wade, one of the guys in my Company, gave me the heads-up."

"Do you believe it's related to my brother?"

"Another ranger *thinks* it's one of the guys in the study."

"Right. No promises."

Get a grip. Slate Thompson had a job. He was doing it, and a side benefit was helping Victor. There was no reason to think any part of it was personal.

No matter how often he held her hand.

Chapter Seven

There is more than one way to kill. There is more than one way to kill. There is more than one way to kill.

Abby wrote in her journal, but scratched each sentence out quickly. She covered it with her hand so no one could see it. Even if she was alone and in a private office.

That didn't matter. The government spied on everyone through all sorts of devices, and the police were everywhere.

Cell phones had cameras. Stoplights had cameras. Cars had back-up cameras. They were everywhere. She couldn't get away from them.

Spies were spies and had to be dealt with. But there was no one around. No one to deal with for the moment.

The doctor had said journals were important. Dr. Roberts had a journal and had written about her as a patient, had written about them all. Abby had taken care of her in the best way she could. Not a perfect way, though. Abby hadn't found that yet.

Dr. Roberts had been right about that particular problem. Abby needed to find it soon. The day was getting close when she'd need to move and start over in another city at another hospital.

"I am not crazy. Dr. Roberts told me I wasn't. I can believe her," she whispered.

Abby needed another pencil. She'd scratched out her last journal sentence so hard, she'd broken the tip. She looked around, but there wasn't another near her to continue. She rolled the chair closer to the small window facing the front of the building.

It was two hours past time to go home. Catching her normal train wouldn't be possible. She was familiar with the alternative, taking a cab, but that wasn't possible either. And she was hungry.

Her subconscious suggestions with Rashad Parker had been so successful that he hadn't waited. He'd gone to the cafeteria, secured a knife and stabbed two people, then slit his throat. Now the hospital was on lockdown.

If she'd known it would work so well, she would have followed him. Now she had been ordered to stay in her office until the hospital was cleared, until the police were certain no one else was at risk.

It was four minutes past dinner.

She moved away from the distracting police lights and arranged the patient binders by date. Then numeric order. She checked the contents to verify that she'd organized them correctly. She'd already finished transcribing the dictation. She listened again. There were no corrections to be made.

She couldn't allow herself to panic just because her schedule was off. She needed to journal more. That would calm the rising nervousness.

A knock on the outer door relieved the moment of panic. She tucked her journal into her handbag with the microtapes she'd used on the sleep-study patients today. She practiced the concerned look she should have in the glass of the only picture hanging on the wall.

The knock persisted. She grabbed her handbag and twisted the lock.

"Come in." She stepped away from the door and waited for the person on the other side to open it.

"Ms. Norman?" The man wasn't dressed like a policeman. He wore a suit and tie.

"Yes. May I go now?"

"Sorry, it's taken a while to clear the offices on each floor. We understand that you had a Rashad Parker here today."

"Yes. He's one of the sleep-study patients. Is he okay? Did something happen?"

"You seem concerned. Was he acting strangely? Make any threats toward anyone?"

"No, of course not." She added a breathiness that indicated worry. She'd studied an emotional thesaurus and practiced at eight o'clock each evening for half an hour. Even so, unable to pursue her normal routine was making her a bit anxious. "May I leave now? I've missed my train and the second train, too."

"I apologize. I forgot to introduce myself. Detective Arnold. Here's my card. I'll have one of the officers escort you out of the building. Mind if I have a look around?"

"I do. I'm not the doctor or the technician. I just set things up for them. There are patient files in here and records. I believe you'll need a court order to proceed with the hospital." She gripped the knob and pulled the door closed behind her. "Which officer will see me safely outside?"

"Burnsy. Will you take Ms. Norman out?"

An officer in full uniform with an automatic weapon took her to the stairs. "Sorry, ma'am, but the elevators are off-limits."

"I prefer the stairs."

On the ground floor, she waited and allowed the officer to open the door—having to remind him that it was the polite thing to do for a lady. She slipped on her surgical gloves and mask for the ride home. She might be forced to take public transportation, but she would not succumb to the germs. She had important work to finish.

Finally out of the building, she took a deep, satisfying breath. There were so many things to add to her study journal. She wished illustrations were possible but her drawings were elementary. She'd never be able to include the images she had in her mind of Dr. Roberts as she died. A shame she hadn't taken actual pictures.

The walk through the sprinkling rain to Lancaster Road let her observe the television reporters, the police and the bystanders. The streets were empty except for those types of vehicles. She sat on her bench next to the Veterans Affairs building at the corner of Avenue of Flags and Liberty Loop, taking a moment to reevaluate.

How would she get to her apartment? Not by sitting here. The light rail train home arrived every fifteen minutes. Police blocked the street and rail entrance but as people came down, they showed their hospital badges and were let by. That's all she had to tell them. She needed by to get home. She had seven more minutes to get on the platform.

A man spoke to both the officers who monitored the road. He showed them a badge. She could hear him offer to help with the situation. But more startled to hear him asking specific questions about Rashid Parker.

"This guy was on my radar and I want to ask the detective in charge to keep me informed. You can understand that, guys, right?"

Abby quickly took out her phone and snapped a picture of the officer. She tried to zoom in on the license plate of the truck he'd gotten out of, but the dimming light and mist made it impossible.

Why is he asking about Rashid?

"Walk past," she whispered behind her mask. "You've missed the train home. You have five minutes and twenty seconds before the next one scheduled. You can control the obsessive-compulsive disorder. You control you. You are not a compulsion." She channeled the last words, repeating them again and again until her feet moved.

Before she allowed herself to think, she showed the police officers her hospital identification. She was even able to pull down the mask so they could verify. She walked through to the next corner, passing the truck, pretending to be absorbed in her phone, but taking pictures of the truck and its occupant.

The woman inside looked familiar. Someone in the study? No. Maybe one of their relatives? She'd look it up when she returned home. She had a file on everyone participating in her study. Knowing everything about them was crucial, including anyone who might care for them and be an outside influence.

But why was a relative at the hospital? And why was she with a police officer? The dark-haired woman was the wrong race to be waiting on news of Rashid.

Her research would give her answers. Reminding herself that today had been excellent, with excellent results. The murder-suicide was the fastest response she'd ever accomplished.

If Abby experienced joy, there would be elation when writing the details of this event. Such a success.

She was one step closer to discovering the perfect death and implementing it on herself.

Chapter Eight

Slate opened the truck door and Vivian jumped from her skin. He climbed inside and chose not to mention that the doors should have been locked even if he was on the outskirts of the taped-off area.

"I couldn't find out much more than what Wade told us. Does the name Rashid Parker mean anything to you?"

"No. Should it?"

"So your brother never mentioned him or anything?"

"My brother barely speaks to me and never about his doctor's murder. It's always events from our childhood, before he joined the army. Does it mean more if he knew Mr. Parker?"

The obvious reason might just be that her brother was guilty. But something told Slate he wasn't. More than Wade's hunch. Something bugged him about Subject Nineteen and the fact that Victor wasn't part of the blind study described in Dr. Roberts's journal.

That had to mean something.

"I look at it this way. I don't like coincidences in any case I work." He was thinking aloud, but being honest with Vivian was essential. "This case has way too many for my comfort level. I'd never hand it over to a prosecutor. I'm surprised the Dallas DA accepted it."

"This feeling of yours—it has something to do with the sleep study?"

"It's sort of a rule of mine. The first itch makes me scratch my head. An investigator might accept one. But then when the second coincidence hits, you're getting into territory that needs another verification. When the third pops up? Well, three coincidences mean something's hinky and your case is about to go to hell."

"Did you discover three?" she asked. "Are you worried about sharing something that might clear my brother? I'll be contacting his attorney whether you do or not."

"That's not a problem. I'll contact him tomorrow." The officer waved them through the intersection and a waft of his sirloin made his stomach growl. "You have steak knives at your place?"

"If not, I give you permission to eat with your fingers."

"Like a wild man. Cool."

"But you still have to explain. What does Rashid Parker have to do with my brother?"

"One. Wade didn't obtain the complete list but he confirmed Parker was at the hospital for the study. Don't ask me how, I'm not asking him. But Parker is definitely a part of the same sleep study that your brother was involved in. Two. None of those men and women are listed as *subject* anything. And three…"

"Yes?"

"Three is that it feels off, too convenient. Why did your brother confess and why has he never been able to recall the details about that day? Everything else, yes, but not that day?" His stomach growled again. "Can you dig me a roll out of the sack?"

"There's a fourth thing." She handed him two fluffy yeast rolls.

"Yeah?"

"The incidents both happened at the VA Hospital."

"Damn, you're right." He inhaled a buttery roll and swallowed. "That's one too many."

"Rolls?"

He laughed. "No. The number of coincidences."

"So do you think they'll let you reopen the case?"

"Hold on a sec." Slate called Wade through his hands-free set, leaving it on speaker so Vivian could hear. "You still at the office, man?"

"Where else am I going to be until these files are done?"

"Forget I asked. Give Heath the necessary info and he'll run his magic on that sleep-study list."

"So my hunch was right?"

"You can lord it over me later." He quickly looked at Vivian. "Call Heath. I need that info before I hit Watts's lawyer's office in the morning."

"I'll get him started. We looking for anything in particular?"

"If I'm right, you'll know." He disconnected as he pulled in front of Vivian's apartment. He could see the hesitation in her body language before she pulled the door handle. "Look, Vivian, I should probably get home."

She visibly relaxed. "Thank you for everything, Slate. I should head inside. I'm working a double tomorrow, so would you leave me a message if you find anything?"

He nodded and pushed the dinner sack at her when she set it in her vacated seat. "You take it. I'll pick up a burger on the way home."

"I can't possibly."

"It's the least I can do for dragging you around in the rain."

Her head shook from side to side. "You aren't going to take no for an answer, are you?"

"I'll stop by the wing place if I find anything."

"Thank you for your help."

"I haven't done anything yet."

Vivian's expression filled with sadness and regret. With that, she shut the truck door. He could read people pretty well and she was silently screaming that she didn't expect anyone—especially a lawman—to help. He waited for her to go inside her apartment, then called Wade again.

"Miss me already?" Wade answered.

"Check with the OIG for the VA. See if they have any weird reports or complaints."

"That would be the Office of Inspector General for Veterans Affairs that won't be open until tomorrow. And what will you be doing?"

"I'm going home and repairing a barn stall like I told

my dad I would. I'm also about to beg my mother to fix me dinner. Totally starved."

"Bring the leftovers tomorrow. Payback for me doing all your legwork."

"You're the one sitting behind a desk, man. I'm the one sitting on wet denim from doing your legwork on this hunch of yours."

"And it's paying off."

"Tomorrow, man."

It was probably better that Vivian Watts had to work a double tomorrow. Probably better since he needed to wrap up his current caseload before he could take vacation days and help her. He couldn't flash around his badge, but mentioning that he was a ranger might open some doors that had been slammed for her.

Statistics weren't in their favor. He wouldn't be just another man who got her hopes up and left her hanging.

Chapter Nine

"I could never have assumed that Rashid would react to the suggestion before he left the hospital." Abby pulled at her cuticles with tweezers. She spoke to the only person completely familiar with her work, herself.

Several doctors, including Roberts, had ordered her to stop, stating it was unhealthy to pick at her nails. They were wrong.

Her skin was raw, but there were still pieces. She picked more furiously before looking up into her red, freshly scrubbed face. Certain there was another layer of dirt on her epidermis, she obtained another washcloth, rubbing and scrubbing as hard as she could.

Setting the cloth onto the counter, she switched back to the tweezers, picking until the bright red of her clean blood seeped around the nail. She went to the cabinet to remove the last washcloth from the sealed bag. She would begin the cleansing process again until she was positive the germs from walking on an unfamiliar street were no longer present.

"Enough!" her reflection yelled.

"I can never get clean enough," she answered behind the cloth.

"You must control yourself, Abby. Break from your routine. There is work to be done. Check the list you made while waiting for the train. It's thorough."

"Yes. I need to identify the woman in the truck." The tweezers caught her eye. She dropped the newer white cloth on top of the metal but immediately had to place them in the sterilizing jar.

"My darling Abby. You are so smart and will find my answers. The perfect death will be ours. I've always had faith in you."

Her encouraging voice from the mirror echoed in her mind as she found her pocket notebook. Flipping the pages, she saw the step-by-step lists of exactly what to do next with her study.

The doctors had all told her that conversing in the mirror wasn't mentally healthy either. They were wrong, too. After talking with the mirror woman, everything was always much clearer.

The goal to merge with her through a perfect death was even more necessary.

She connected her laptop to the external memory, careful to remain free from the internet. Her research on each of the sleep-study veterans confirmed her suspicion. The woman in the truck was the sister of Victor Watts. She'd almost forgotten about the young man.

What was the sister doing with an officer at Rashid's death? What about another veteran's death would pique the curiosity of a family member from the sleep study?

The voice in the mirror, both perfect and sterile,

was right again. Follow the steps, follow the lists she'd already written. She could concentrate on the list and avoid the problems culminating from her disrupted day.

Even though her schedule had changed, it was deeply satisfying news that Rashid had reacted so quickly. A very hopeful sign that her experiments were working even better.

So what if family were curious. She had a plan already in place to take care of anything or anyone who might upset her goals. One phone call would activate him to perform whatever deed needed. He'd taken care of problems before and never remembered. He could take care of this, too.

Many times she'd been to doctors, trying to overcome the debilitating obsessive compulsions that sidetracked her from completing her work. They'd all failed, concentrating instead on the one thing that made her focus, gave her clarity. Attempting to take away the voice in the mirror wasn't right. The perfect voice that brought precision to her thoughts.

The voice was serenity. The voice was excellence.

The voice was necessary.

Vivian Watts…was not.

Chapter Ten

Vivian savored every bite of half a steak. She carefully wrapped the other portion in foil and stuck it in the freezer. Then she packed her laptop and caught a bus for the nearest free Wi-Fi.

She hadn't given Slate the only copy of the study. He might not have vocalized all his thoughts, but she caught on pretty quick. The other thing she could do was research.

She didn't trust that Slate or the others would get the complete list of participants, but it couldn't be that difficult to find them. There had to be some way to narrow down the sleep-study list. It was easier than anticipated since it was specifically focused on veterans. Then it became apparent that nothing had happened to the females in the study, but the guys were a different story.

The study was in two parts, one prior to Dr. Roberts's death and another after. The results had been published in recent medical journals so Roberts's coworkers could continue the research. There were sixty participants— thirty of each gender. But no names.

The search she conducted was the first that came to

her mind…murders by veterans limited to the previous year. Some had been seen at the VA Hospital, including her brother. Without much specific information, she couldn't be certain, but it looked as if the number of incidents involving local veterans had dramatically increased.

"Why hasn't anyone looked into this?" she mumbled in total shock. Rashid Parker was the fourteenth man she'd found in the surrounding area.

She dug through her purse, looking for Slate's card. The announcement that the library would close in a few minutes had already been made. She saved all the pages of research as screenshots, printed and put them in a folder to work with at home.

The phone call to Slate would have to wait until her break the next day. The card gave his office and cell numbers but she didn't really have any information for him. What could she pass along? She'd wait for the half-hour break she'd get between her shifts at the restaurant.

Once home, she packed her suitcase just in case the landlord decided to act on the last day of the month instead of the morning of the first. She retrieved a second suitcase from the closet with the few possessions her brother had. Laptop and valuables were in a smaller bag that she'd take with her and store under the counter—whether the chicken manager liked it or not.

She'd sold her car, sold her possessions in Florida and felt like she'd hit rock bottom. But each time she thought about herself, she remembered the eleven months her brother had been in jail. Eleven months of suffering, of defending himself, of thinking he'd killed the doctor that he'd spoken so highly of.

According to Victor, Dr. Roberts was going to "fix" him, "cure" him. The plan was that he'd participate in her study and she'd know exactly how his brain ticked. And if they knew that…the night terrors would stop.

Vivian had never understood why he'd harm the only person who had given him hope. The one doctor who could take his nightmares away. She'd mentioned that to his lawyer with every visit. After a month, she no longer had access to discuss her brother's case. The lawyer wouldn't see her. She had no legal recourse. No access to any discovery or evidence the prosecutor had obtained.

In the dark. No legal recourse to fight for her brother. The second and current attorneys had refused to discuss the case with her at all.

There it was again. The flicker of hope shone like a bright star in the sky, twinkling just out of her reach. Slate didn't seem like a person who would flicker out. He was more the type who provided secure warmth like the sun.

She fell sleep. Her dreams of being a young child playing with her brother in a warm field quickly changed to the sun burning her skin. The feeling that she was lying on the ground had her twisting. Somehow she knew it was the padding that tried to pass for a mattress. She was asleep, but then she wasn't.

Police cars. Firefighters. Loud sirens and lights. She was dreaming. It felt like a war documentary. Something from World War I. Loud cracking, explosions, gas masks, shouting. She wanted to wake up.

"Don't struggle. We got you!" The voice came through a fog.

Stuck between dreams and waking, she struggled to understand the man's words through his gas mask. She didn't like the dream and struggled more. She twisted round and round in the sheets, tangling them around her legs until she was paralyzed. She couldn't move. Couldn't breathe.

She needed to wake up before she died.

"Miss. Miss!" A hand on her shoulder shook her awake.

Vivian opened her eyes, an oxygen mask on her face. She coughed, wanting to sit, but she was strapped to a gurney and couldn't move.

She shook her head. "Let me up," she said under the plastic.

"Sure. Are you injured? Do you know where you are?"

The men around her looked like paramedics. Each unbuckled a strap and she was free.

"What happened?" She pushed up to a sitting position, coughing the entire way.

"The whole apartment building is in flames," someone cried behind her. "They're still getting people out."

"Do they...do they know how it started?"

"Not yet."

She swung her feet to the side until they hit the ground. The paramedic handed her the oxygen and didn't take no for an answer, pushing it to cover her nose and mouth.

The dream made sense now. She hadn't been in World War I with rescuers and masks hiding their faces. She'd been in a fire. The major portion of the blaze was at her apartment. She watched the men battling inside and out of the tiny place that had been her home.

Oh, my God. It couldn't have started with her. Nothing had been on, not even the heater. So what had happened?

The paramedic draped the blanket over her shoulders. She gripped it around her neck like a protective cloak. *Pajamas. Thank God she'd been wearing them.*

She watched, helpless. There was no going back to her brother's apartment. Her living space. Gone. Everything she owned was inside. Gone.

"You're so lucky you faced the street. They knocked down your door first. I watched them pull you out. I thought you were dead." A woman stood next to her dressed in a long robe and slippers.

Dressed as she was, Vivian assumed she was one of the neighbors who'd had to abandon their home, too. "Are you okay? Need to sit down?"

"No. I was out walking my dog." She opened a flap of her robe and flashed the face of a small Chihuahua. "Me and Bohemian are just fine. We live on the other side of the block." She pointed down the street as she clasped the dog and covered him with the thick robe.

"Do you have a phone?"

"Sure. Call anyone you like, honey. I sure hope someone can come get you since you ain't getting back into that apartment." She pointed to the burned-out hollow where she'd been sleeping. "You are really lucky to be alive."

"I think so, too."

She tapped for Information. "Do you have a number for a local Texas Ranger's office? I think he said it was in Garland."

Chapter Eleven

"You brought her here? Home?" Heath Murray asked from his bedroom doorway. "Doesn't this break a ton of rules or something?"

Slate had been awakened by the emergency phone call from his office. It took him over an hour to find Vivian, who'd been taken to a local emergency room. "Where else do you suggest I take her? She refused to go to a hotel and insisted on a women's shelter."

"It's better than hiding the truth from the major." Slate's roommate stood in his boxers, squinting from the lack of contacts, hair standing straight out from his head. "What's wrong with the women's shelter?"

"She'd be eaten alive there." He lowered his voice and took a step closer to his friend. "She's got nothing, man. Every penny she had, her phone, her laptop…all gone."

"I can hear you," Vivian said, standing between the kitchen and the living room. "And I did tell him to take me to a shelter. He's the one who's being stubborn about this."

Slate turned back to her. "Honestly, it's not a big deal.

I don't know why Heath's so bent out of shape. You're staying here tonight and that's the end of it."

"Well, since I'm sort of stranded, I have no choice. But I'm definitely the one sleeping on the couch." Her fingers clung to the blanket the EMTs had provided. Her feet were barely protected with hospital or crime scene paper booties. She was probably in shock, and yet she stood straight and undefeated.

"Please take his room," Heath said, throwing up his hands. "If you don't, I'm never getting back to sleep."

Slate slapped him on his bare shoulder. "Since you're up…"

"I'm not." Heath took his skinny legs and bare feet back down the hall. "I'm not up. Figment of your imagination walking here."

Slate didn't watch him go. He just waited for the door to slam. It did.

"I'm taking the couch and you're staying in my room. It also has a private bath so you can get cleaned up. You breathing okay? They told me to watch out for wheezing."

"I should never have called you. I only did in case you tried to find me with news about Victor's case and the person answering the phone insisted I give a reason."

"I'm glad you called."

"I think someone deliberately set that fire."

He was taken off guard that Vivian had said it. Not that the thought hadn't already been in his head since the moment she got a hold of him.

"Yeah, one too many coincidences. But why now?

They've had months to do something like this. Why wait until I poked my nose into it?"

"I went to the library after you dropped me off and began my own research."

"And?" He leaned against the wall, growing conscious of the dirty ranch clothes he'd thrown on to go find her.

"I didn't have anything definitive. Nothing except a rise in violent behavior from veterans. Out of the fourteen news articles I read, at least half the relatives mentioned they thought the accused had been getting better since seeking treatment at the hospital."

"Parker would make fifteen and your brother would be another. Sixteen men? All veterans? What time frame are we looking at?"

"I went back a year before I ran out of time. I don't think you can call it a coincidence, Slate."

"You went back to your apartment after the library. Was anyone acting suspicious or seem to be following you?"

"No. It was another hour or so before I got ready for bed. I wanted everything packed and ready to leave with me." She pursed her lips together, a classic tell that she thought she'd said too much to him.

"Leave?"

"Oh, my gosh, I might as well tell you since you're going to find out anyway." She sat on the couch, resting her elbow on the arm and rubbing her temple with her fingers. "Victor's lease is up and I couldn't sign a new one. The manager increased the rent three times and told me he didn't want me staying. So you might as well take me to the shelter. I'm going to be living there anyway."

"You couldn't afford to find another place?"

"I spent everything I had on cheap private detectives who didn't connect any dots. You've gotten further in one day just looking at a sleep-study report."

"I have special resources."

"I plan on returning to Miami after the trial next week. I'll try to get a job with the firm I worked for before all this began. I'm not sure if they'll take me back, but they at least said to contact them."

How much more bad luck could this woman take?

"And what do you plan on doing until then?" Slate could assume what the answer was. The thoughts running through his head went against everything he'd worked for, trained for. "You can't be serious about staying in the shelter?"

"It's conveniently located near the courthouse and jail." She dropped her head to the back of the couch. "Don't worry about me. I'll be fine."

"What about your job? That's a long way by bus and DART."

"Tomorrow—I mean, today was my last day. The manager wouldn't give me time off for Victor's trial. Do you think anything survived the fire?"

She was on the verge of tears and collapse. Did she even realize she'd almost died? There was a high probability that someone had tried to kill her.

"We'll take a look as soon as they give the go-ahead to get back in," Slate promised.

"Oh, for the love of Pete, man. Ask her already," Heath yelled from his room.

Slate turned to Vivian and covered her hand resting on the sofa. "Please take my room. You do *not* want to face him walking around in the morning. He's a jackass before coffee."

"Ask me what?"

"Good grief, I'll say it." Heath stuck his head out between the door and wall. "She can stay here and I'll keep my mouth shut about it. No one from the Company will know. But I need sleep. Please go to bed."

"I can't possibly stay here. You know nothing about me and can't open your home like this."

"Look, this is easier than it seems. You can stay in the guest bunkhouse. My family runs a sort of dude ranch and gives riding lessons. We'll get you set up tomorrow. But for now, Heath's right. You need sleep. Come on."

He gently tugged her hand and the rest of her body followed.

"I don't like giving in."

"Consider it a compromise. Both of us win."

"Even me if I can get some sleep," Heath said sarcastically as they passed his door.

"I'm truly sorry. I didn't mean to be a bother."

Slate closed his bedroom door behind them so his roommate could get back to sleep. Vivian's voice shook like she was close to being hysterical or she was heading into shock. She also smelled like the fire. Smoke clung to her clothes and even her hair, which was loose and curly around her shoulders.

"Through there. Clean towels in the cabinet." He pointed. He went to the bathroom door and opened it, gesturing for her to go through.

Vivian didn't move. At least her feet didn't. Her hands covered her face and the dam of tears broke. She cried silently into her palms. He watched her shoulders shake and her upper body begin to fold downward to her knees.

He did the only thing a good ol' country boy could... caught her to him.

Holding her, it didn't matter how late it was or that she smelled like smoke. All there was right then was defending Vivian from anything else crappy happening to her. She was right that he barely knew her. But she'd given up everything for her brother.

Everything.

That type of loyalty was worth staying up all night to help save.

"It'll be okay, Vivian. Go ahead and cry. Get it out. You'll be okay."

THE STRONG ARMS wrapped around her gave Vivian a sense of belonging she hadn't had since Victor left for his tour overseas. But this wasn't her brother.

It was a stranger who had quickly become her lifeline. Her only lifeline that was keeping her from fending for herself on the street. It had been a while since someone showed her so much kindness.

The more she thought about it, the more she cried. The more she cried, the tighter Slate held her. She pushed at his chest trying to back away... He cupped the back of her head and encouraged her cheek to rest on his chest.

She didn't care. If he'd hold her longer, she'd let him. Everything was just so… She didn't have the energy to think how desperate her situation had become. The tears tapered off and she could finally get herself under control. Her body was aware of the strong muscles under her hands and against her torso. Naturally muscled from hard work and sweat.

Slate smelled of smoke, hay and clean dirt. His skin had a natural muskiness that completely matched the nice-cowboy image he portrayed.

The smoke, she soon realized, was totally her. Remnants of a building burning around her. *Oh, my gosh.*

"If someone wanted to kill me, they didn't have to follow me home. They already knew where I stayed because that's where Victor lived when Dr. Roberts was murdered."

"That makes sense." He leaned back, looking at her and swallowing hard like he was confused. "You ready for that shower now? I don't have any flowery soap, but you'll get clean."

"Yeah, I probably should." She stepped back and then turned around, catching a huge whiff of smoke into her lungs.

The visceral reminder of how she'd narrowly escaped hit her. In fact, she hadn't really escaped at all. Whoever called 911 for help—and the sheer luck that her door faced the street—had brought the firefighters to her rescue first.

"I'll be fast." She had to get the smoke off her. Now.

She marched to the bathroom, shut and locked the door, then turned only the hot water on. Steam began building up immediately. She coughed and coughed, clearing her lungs until she could breathe easier. Then washed her hair until she lost count of the number of rinses it took to get the smell out of it.

Afterward, she dried with a fluffy yellow towel that matched the bath decor and wrapped it tightly around herself.

It was a small bath of soft yellows and blue and the steam seemed to turn to smoke. It was just her imagination. She'd been unconscious for the entire incident. She didn't have any memories of the actual fire. It didn't make sense that she could know it wasn't real and still panic.

That didn't matter.

The fear of being trapped in a burning building surrounded her, taking over any logic she'd ever maintained. She burst out of the small room, unable to catch her breath.

"Oh, my…God. I…" she huffed. She cupped her hands over her mouth like Slate had that afternoon but couldn't keep them there.

The closed bedroom door opened, banging against some western gear. Slate took one look at her and pulled her to him. His calloused hand, stuck between his shirt and her lips, didn't let any air to her lungs, forcing her to slow her rapid intake through her nose.

He held her tightly but managed to tilt her eyes to look at him. Holding her gaze, he counted in a whisper.

"Fourteen, fifteen, sixteen, ninety-two, ninety-three. Count with me, Vivian."

"Ninety-four, ninety-five," she mumbled under his fingers.

"That's right. Six, seven, eight," he began.

"Nine, ten, eleven." She stopped, breathing easier if not completely normal.

"You're good, now?" He hugged her tight, then shifted his hands to cup her shoulders. "Two in one day. You said you've never had this happen before? Back up a bit, darlin'. Yeah, just like that." He guided her elbows. "Okay. There. Sit. You're right by the bed."

"I'm okay," she managed in spite of the heavy wheezing. "I don't know what's wrong."

"Now's not the time to think about it. You should squeeze between these covers and try to get some rest. Your body will feel better in the morning."

"I...I can't." She self-consciously tucked the towel tighter, unsure what she could ever think about that would make her close her eyes again.

"Is a T-shirt okay? I'll wash your stuff in a minute." He patted her clumsily on the back.

The man hadn't hesitated when he'd flattened her to his body to stop the hyperventilating. Now his awkward hesitation brought a smile to her lips. He took out a clean—almost starched—white T-shirt and placed it in her hands. Did a double take, then switched it out for a dark navy.

"I'll see you in the morning."

The door shut and she was alone. She dressed, hung

the towel over the shower bar and dropped her head onto a pillow that reminded her of comfort and safety.

It smelled just like Slate.

Chapter Twelve

"Your problem's having another nightmare, man." Heath kicked Slate's foot that had fallen off the end of the couch. "Time to get up anyway."

No daylight came through the windows. Just the light above the coffee maker had been flipped on. In the moment it took Slate to register why he was on the couch, he heard Vivian's cries.

"My problem?"

Heath was dressed for ranch duties. "I still can't believe you let Wade talk you into helping him. You know what happened when Jack helped."

Slate sat up, scratching his head. "Hell, Heath. Jack got a commendation from the state."

"I mean Wade's on desk duty. If he's caught working on this…he's done."

Vivian cried out again. Slate headed her direction.

"Just think hard before you dig yourself—and Wade—into a deeper hole."

Slate knocked softly on the door, waiting to see if Vivian would settle down or wake up. There was no reason for her to wake up as early as him and the other ranch hands. He'd rather have a plan of action in place, too. But it didn't matter.

Vivian alternated between a whimper and a cry. It was obvious she was having a nightmare. He peeked inside the door and saw that the sheets were caught around her legs. Her hair was tangled around her neck. Her face was damp with sweat.

He left her momentarily and retrieved a damp rag, a bottle of water and a robe that his mother had given to him three Christmases ago. Rarely worn and long enough to cover her better than the T-shirt.

God, he was glad he'd switched the color. As he approached the bed, he could see only the outline of her breasts through the dark blue instead of embarrassing her with see-through white.

"Vivian." He touched her foot a little more gently than Heath had kicked his. "Hey, Miss Watts. Time to wake up. Everything's okay."

"What?" Her eyes popped open wide and she immediately began to cough.

He twisted off the water bottle top and stuck the bottle out in front of her. She nodded her head, dripping with sweat like she'd actually been in a fire. He moved to the side of the bed and knelt to her eye level.

"You okay?"

"Where—oh, right, the fire. What time is it?" She tugged at the sheets, then the T-shirt. "I'd get dressed, but pajamas aren't going to get me very far."

"I'll throw them in the dryer in a minute. I do have this robe." He patted the end of the bed, then handed her the damp cloth. "And this."

"Thanks. Slate, you're being far too kind. Maybe you can take me to the shelter. I'm sure they have clothes but I might need to borrow something to get there."

Grateful and definitely independent.

"Sure…on the clothes. No to the women's shelter." He checked his phone. "We don't need to go over this again. Okay? It'll be easier on everyone if you're close by. I need to call Wade and the office. Be right back."

Dialing the number, he left the room before she could object again.

"This better be good," Wade said, sounding asleep.

"I thought you'd be up and on your way to the office. In fact, get your butt up. I need some answers."

"Answers for what exactly?"

"I need to know if arson is suspected in a fire."

"I'll need more details than that. Like where and why do you suspect arson?"

"I believe someone tried to kill Vivian Watts last night. Her apartment building caught fire around midnight. Fortunately, no one was injured."

"If you were trying to get me out of bed the same ungodly hour that you do, you've done it. Now stop kidding around."

"No joke, man. She lost everything. I picked her up from the hospital—"

"What do you mean, *you* picked her up?"

"She didn't have anybody else. Look, I'm taking a few days off to check this out. But you've got to do some legwork with the police, fire, et cetera."

"So the hunch was right?"

"No time to gloat, man. Get me some answers. I gotta go feed the horses."

He cut off the call during Wade's next word. "I need coffee," he muttered to himself. "I think I'll even drink Heath's strong stuff this morning."

The smoke-scented clothes he'd slept in would be good enough for barn work. He filled his travel mug, yanked on his boots and headed outside. First light, and Heath was already saddled and working his mare in the paddock.

Slate climbed to the top of the fence and watched, sipping coffee that he normally watered down. A lack of sleep and the need to think a bit faster this morning got him used to the thick-as-mud mixture pretty quickly.

"Stardust is looking pretty good there, Heath. You taking her this weekend?" Slate's dad asked his roommate, then turned to greet him. "Morning, son."

"Morning, Dad."

Heath eased up the mare and sauntered her to the fence where Slate's dad was leaning.

"Naw. Probably withdrawing this weekend, sir. I think my caseload just got heavier."

Heath cut him an I-can't-believe-you're-pulling-this look.

His dad turned to him. "You pulling out, too, son? That mean your mother and me can take off to the casino?"

"Yeah, I'll be around to take care of things."

"If you can't, your sister will be around to give her lessons. Hot diggity." His sixty-year-old father did his version of an Irish jig with muddy boots and his jeans tucked inside them. Then a quick look back to Heath. "Sorry you won't be competing, guys. But we have this free weekend stay and upgrade at the casino in Oklahoma."

"Don't worry about things here, Dad." Slate jumped from the top rung. "I better get started. Hey, is Mom up?"

"Is that a real question?" His dad slapped the wood rail. "You boys want breakfast?"

"Early morning for me, sir." Heath took Stardust around the paddock again. "Thanks anyway."

Slate nodded. "Let me feed the horses and I'll be right up."

"Mind getting the gate?" Heath asked.

Slate walked the same direction as his roommate while his dad headed back to the house. "Before you say a damn word. Yes, I'm going to tell him I've got a guest. There's no reason to keep it a secret."

"I was just going to remind you that it's very possible someone attempted to kill your *guest* last night and you might warn your dad to sleep with his gun loaded while she's here."

Slate laughed. "No need to tell him to do something he's already doing. But I'll mention it." He closed the gate behind his partner, watching him ride into the field.

Finishing his chores, he texted Wade for an update as he scrapped his boots outside the back door of his mom's kitchen.

One word came back: ARSON.

Had he brought danger into his parents' lives? Stupid question. Of course he had, by bringing an unknown back to his home. He'd never once thought that his law-enforcement career would put anyone at risk other than himself. He was helping, bringing justice to the innocent.

Did that trump safety? *Dammit.*

Not only did Vivian's brother need him to find the real murderer, he now needed to protect his family. Solving this case fast benefited everyone.

He'd need more background on Vivian, her brother, the victim and who benefited from the doctor's death. All things Wade could look up. He texted him to ask. Wade responded with another one-word answer: DUH.

The smells of bacon, fresh biscuits and eggs drifted through the screen door. The smell alone made his stomach long for food.

"Morning, Slate. Dad said you might want breakfast." His mom opened her arms for a hug.

"Yes, ma'am. Got extra?"

"You been smoking cigars again, son? You smell all smoky." She turned back to her skillet of scrambled eggs. "I thought Heath didn't want anything."

"Actually, I have a houseguest."

"Oh." His mother's voice singsonged a variety of notes, which was a signal that she approved. "This is almost done."

"It's not like that. I was checking out a hunch about this murder case and the accused's sister was in a fire last night. She didn't have anywhere else to go."

"So you brought her here. That's admirable."

"Well, I thought so. Until I found out someone's probably trying to kill her."

His mom faced him with both hands on her hips. "You're worried about me and your dad? Or do you need our help?"

"Yes and no. I think it's a good idea that you're leaving for a long weekend. I'm sure I'll have all this cleared up by the time you get back Sunday night."

He better. The trial began Monday morning. That was less than a week.

"I'm sure your dad will take whatever precautions you think are necessary. We'll leave first thing in the morning. That'll give you four days. In the meantime, I'll let you take breakfast home so she won't have to deal with meeting us today." She set out plastic containers with enough breakfast to feed four people.

Mainly because she knew Heath would eat no matter how many times he told her it wasn't necessary to give him food. She enjoyed cooking…so why not let her? But she also included Slate's guest without him asking.

"You're a great mom. You know that, right?" He kissed her upturned cheek.

"And you're a good son. Now, what else do you need?"

Slate grabbed a slice of crisp bacon, shoving it in his mouth quickly before his mom snatched it back. "Clothes. Any of Sophia's laundry still here?"

"I'll get it along with some clean towels. I'm sure you boys are running low." She wiped her hands on her apron, heading to the laundry. "There's an extra jacket hanging by the door. It should fit unless your guest is as tall as you."

"Vivian." He opened his containers, put bacon and

eggs on a biscuit and took three bites between words. "Her name's Vivian Watts. And she's not tall. Barely reaches my shoulders."

"Well, I look forward to meeting her. Will you be in for supper?"

"Don't count on it, Mom. This isn't a social stay."

"There's no reason to be rude, kiddo. I'll make sure your fridge is stocked with girl food. You know, something that's fresh and not frozen." She set the food containers on top of the laundry basket and placed it in his hands.

"I'm serious, Mom. She'll probably want her privacy. She's going through a rough time right now."

"She was in a fire, sweetie. I figured out the rough time on my own." She held the screen door open and waved him through. "I'm a phone call or text away. All I'm doing is cleaning my sewing room today so if you need me…I'm here."

"Thanks. And thanks for breakfast."

"Don't eat it all before you share it." She let the screen close and he heard her mumble, "I swear it's like I never taught him any manners at all."

"THE NEWS SAID no one was injured in the fire. My building isn't habitable any longer. All those people are homeless because of me."

"Not your fault," Slate said with his full mouth, doing his best not to be rude.

"I had already packed the few things Victor and I had left. Do you think they were destroyed?"

"We'll check." He kicked the door closed and went to the kitchen.

"Where's your roommate? The one who thinks I'm a problem."

"He didn't mean that." Slate unloaded the basket he'd returned with. "You hungry? Mom made breakfast."

"I didn't realize your parents live here. Look, if someone tried to kill me, then I should leave for the shelter. You can't argue with me about this any longer."

"You're staying. My parents are aware."

"You have to stop being so kind," she whispered.

She would have left an hour ago if she'd had money to pay a cab. Or shoes. Or even pants. Instead, she'd stayed with no phone. No laptop. Nothing to do except become more paranoid and aware of the burden she would become if she stayed.

Taking advantage of Slate's generosity was problematic. Nothing good could become of it.

"Mom sent some of Sophia's things. My sister has a habit of starting her laundry and not hanging around until it's finished. To tell you the truth—" he took a bite of a biscuit "—I think my mom secretly enjoys folding it all up for her. Sure beats cleaning horse stalls."

Slate faced her with jeans, T-shirts and a jacket. "I figured we could stop by a store later to get you a couple of pairs of shoes and other stuff you need."

Vivian didn't need a mirror to tell her what he was thinking. She concentrated on slowing her breath so she wouldn't lose it. No more hyperventilating. There wasn't a reason to react to kindness with a panic attack.

She drew a deep breath through her nose and let it out through her mouth.

"You want to eat or get dressed first?"

"It's the unknown." She couldn't ignore the fact that she was fighting to maintain control. "I'm so sorry. I don't want to be a charity case. I don't know when I'll ever be able to repay you."

Slate took plates out of the cabinet, added food and gestured for her to sit at the small round dining table. He handed her a fork before getting salt and pepper. Then he poured two cups of coffee before he joined her.

Vivian tugged her robe's belt tighter and made certain there weren't any gaps. She was starved and the food smelled delicious. Slate didn't wait for her to take a bite. He seasoned his eggs, buttered his biscuits and ate.

"You okay?"

She nodded.

"I'm not sure what's the best way to get out of this situation. I kept thinking that a better job would come through. I was handling things paycheck to paycheck until the landlord decided he wanted me out."

"Let's just take a day at a time. After I shower, we'll check out your apartment, talk with the fire marshal, see what's what. Then we decide what comes next." He set his elbows on either side of his plate. "It'll be easier for me and my team if you stay with me. If you insist on the shelter, that means I'll be cranky from the crick in my neck."

"I don't understand."

"You staying at the shelter means I'm awake most of the night watching the place from my truck. Then

Heath's even moodier, since I'm sure to twist his arm into helping me. It's better on all of us if you can stay here. See? It's really a very selfish plan."

She doubted that.

"Is your roommate in law enforcement, too? I thought he was a ranch hand or something. Didn't he go riding?"

"Heath works and trains his mares every morning before being a Texas Ranger. He pays Mom and Dad a lower boarding fee by living here and helping out on the ranch. Every other weekend, he rodeos. He more than earns his keep and even helps out with giving riding lessons."

"He seemed upset that you brought me here."

"He'll get over it. Mind putting that away while I get cleaned up?" He pointed to the food.

"Not at all."

While Slate got ready for the day, she tidied up, then hurried into the borrowed clothes. There was a laptop sitting on the coffee table, but she couldn't bring herself to invade the privacy of whoever owned it. She'd be patient.

Time may be running out. But after waiting eleven months for someone to help—or even care—she could wait another hour.

Chapter Thirteen

Arson. The thought had crossed her mind. Even though she'd brought up the possibility, she still didn't want to believe it. Slate was speaking with the Dallas fire marshal and an arson investigator while she waited in his truck.

On the bright side, Slate's sister seemed to be taller, but was basically the same size. Heath had delivered a variety of clothing when he returned from his ride. He'd apologized for being rude or wary of her arrival, as he'd put it. At least she didn't have to find free clothes.

Or shoes. Slate had taken her to a store and wouldn't let her go inside alone. Each time she picked one thing out, he put three in the cart. He'd spent way too much money, but she'd stashed the receipt in the small purse he'd chosen while she was in the dressing room.

Her emotions were still bouncing everywhere. Hard to control—harder still to predict. The urge to feel sorry for herself was overwhelming. She really wanted to give in by binge-watching a series and eating a bag of chips and salsa.

Adding to that self-pity was the fact that she didn't

have a couch or bed to crawl under the covers and watch anything. But she wasn't a poor-poor-pitiful-me girl. She and her brother had faced hardships before. They could overcome this situation, too.

Slate walked around her apartment building with his hands in his pockets. He'd taken his Texas Ranger star with him, showed it to the two men he was speaking with and then dropped it inside his shirt pocket. He'd mentioned during the drive that his involvement would need to be low-key. She wanted to join him, to look at everything, hear the words of the inspectors and see if anything had survived.

The desire to walk the seventy or so feet to her former apartment and pull her suitcases from the fire remains was significant. So much so that she had her seat belt off and the door slightly ajar. She could overhear Slate coaxing the officials. Promising to give them any information he and she discovered. Assuring them that if she were the intended target, she was safer in his custody than anywhere else.

The contents of her apartment had been cleared, since the fire had definitely been set on the outside of the building. She had her doubts about whether the laptop or phone would work again. Everything she or her brother owned would reek of smoke, but at least they'd have something.

A head nod from one of the guys, and Slate walked directly to her two suitcases. He jerked them up like they were empty. Straight out of the mud and muck that now covered everything. She shut her door as he tossed them into the back of the truck.

"They don't have any idea who set the fire. It's not unusual that no one sees anything or wants to get involved. Whoever it was…complete amateur. They had no experience, according to the investigator. Didn't try to make the flames big or anything."

"From here, it just looked like one corner was burned." She stretched to see if either suitcase was black. Neither was; they were just very dirty from the firefighters putting out the flames.

"That's right. They poured gasoline on the ground around the natural gas line, left the can and drove away. It's only about ten feet from the parking lot."

"And at that time of night and in the rain, no one would think to be watching out their window."

"Right. But at least we have a place to start," he said and lifted the corner of his mouth in a teasing grin.

"No one saw anything. I don't understand."

"Whatever we did yesterday caught someone's attention."

"I know this isn't in my wheelhouse like yours, but I still don't see where that gets us."

"Trust me."

"Where are we going now?"

"I made an appointment this time with your brother's lawyer, told him it was about payment. That should get him in the office. Then we'll head to the VA Hospital." He turned the wheel, heading in the same direction as the day before.

At least he'd gotten an appointment. The attorney had refused to see her several times, always stating that

Victor didn't want her involved. When had she lost her tenacity? Her determination?

When had she allowed herself to be so defeated?

"Don't you have work?"

"I took a few days off."

She was in a far bigger debt to Slate Thompson than he could ever know or that she could ever repay. He was helping a stranger, giving her hope and courage. She was about to tell him exactly that when his hand covered hers.

"This has got to be hard on you. I have a feeling you've been doing everything yourself. For the record, do you and your brother have any other family?"

She shook her head. "This part of our story always seems to convince the police or lawyers that Victor is guilty. We're a product of the system. I was raised by a normal foster-care family. My brother is five years younger and was placed in a different home. I managed to see him about once every three months or so. It got to where his foster family wouldn't allow us much time on the phone or especially together."

"So everyone thinks he's a bad product of a bad system."

"That's the nice way to say it." Vivian nervously rubbed the tops of her thighs. "Without anything— family, friends, a support system or money—our only option for a college degree was the army. By the time Victor turned eighteen, he'd had enough of school. He took his GED and left for boot camp."

"Wait." He looked at her like he was confused. "You were in the army? You can shoot a gun?"

"Can't you?" she asked.

"Yeah, but I'm better with a shotgun. I almost had to bribe someone during the last qualification."

He had to be kidding.

He chuckled. "Aw, yes. I've seen your level of confusion before. A Texan, raised on a ranch, who can't shoot? Okay, so I'm pulling your leg a bit. It's not far from the truth. Continue."

"I'd been saving money and had no intention of letting him enlist, but he did it while I was overseas. We didn't see each other for about six years. Oh, we wrote more often in the beginning. But the emails got fewer and took longer to send. Part of that time, I was in school at Florida State. Other times, I didn't know what part of Afghanistan Victor had been assigned to. He mustered out in San Antonio, opting to stay in Texas to work with Dr. Roberts and her sleep study."

"The file said he had night terrors. That's from the army?"

"Yes. Pretty bad ones, from what I understand. But that doesn't mean he's a murderer."

"Agreed. It doesn't."

The sun left his tanned face as he pulled the truck into a parking garage. She'd been so engrossed in the telling of her and Victor's story that they'd arrived at the attorney's office building without her realizing.

"Let's go see if we can find a place to start."

It didn't take long to walk from the parking garage into the sleek glass building. The Public Defender's Office was located at the county courthouse, but Victor's lawyer was assigned by the court and in Uptown. The door to the office was locked and no one was inside. It wasn't unusual.

"Does he have a receptionist?"

"The building might be nice, but in the past several months, I've never seen anyone working with or for attorney Ned Stevens," she explained to Slate.

He knelt at the door. At first she thought he was tying his shoe or something, but remembered he wore boots. Then he pulled out a small pocket-size case. "I am certain that breaking and entering is illegal in all fifty states, Slate. Some places in the world they even cut off your hands. You're an officer of the law. You should know that."

"I'm tired of this guy never being in his office when he says he will be." He twisted pick tools in the lock.

"Why do you even have those tools?" she whispered.

"Funny story. I was a resident assistant in college and—"

"Someone's coming. Your funny story will have to wait."

Slate slid his tools back in his jacket and they stood with their backs against the door, waiting for the footsteps to advance from around the corner.

"Anyway, these two freshman football players got it in their head to change the locks on my floor," Slate continued.

"As in the doorknobs?" Vivian asked.

A nicely dressed woman, carrying a briefcase, came into view and passed them.

Slate acknowledged the passerby with a nod of his head. "Crazy, right?"

"It doesn't make sense. No one could do that."

"They could if they had a master key to the building." He knelt down, pulling out his two picks.

"You are not going to continue with this? Slate!" she whisper-shouted. "People are returning from court or lunch or wherever. Let's just wait for Mr. Stevens."

"No time. Keep your ears open."

"We have…" she bent next to him "…no other pressing appointments."

"We only have five days." He stuck picks back into the lock. "I imagine there are a lot of names on that list to check. We need to see what's in your brother's file. Today."

She cupped his shoulder. "Slate. This isn't the way."

They stood. His eyes darted around her face. Hers probably did the same since she caught all the small crinkle lines near his eyes and the corner of his mouth. A tiny lift began on the left side of his mouth, then stopped. His lips parted slightly and she caught a whiff of coffee.

She didn't mind. He smelled good.

Wait a minute! How did they get so close? He was practically a head taller than she was and yet somehow his eyes were now at her level. That meant so was his mouth. Their position shifted as subtly as his smile.

One step forward, and his hands were planted on either side of her shoulders. He tilted his head and gently pressed his lips against hers. She did what any sane woman in her place would do…she kissed him back.

Her arms were at her sides, but that didn't stop them from reaching out and sliding around his waist to his back. Her fingers didn't meet anything soft. Muscles were rock hard across his sides and under his jacket. His freshly pressed shirt was crisp under her fingertips.

One of his hands dropped to her shoulder as her lips parted and he swirled his tongue next to hers. Was she still thinking? Or just absorbing every tantalizing feeling coursing through her body.

"Miss Watts?"

She jerked her head to the right where the voice had spoken. "Mr. Stevens. Sorry, you caught us…off… off…"

"You caught us." Slate winked and made a clicking noise like he might be telling a horse to move. She stared at him while pushing at his chest with her left hand. He moved in slow motion, one hand dropping to her hip instead of pulling away completely. Did he want—

He did. The sincere look, the kiss, the touches…it was all to…to what? Catch her off guard or Ned Stevens?

"Slate Hansom." He finally moved his body and stuck his hand out to shake Ned's.

"For real? Oh, sorry. Of course you're real. I'm…" Keys out, Victor's attorney pointed to the door. "I need…let me just open this." Ned squeezed between them. "Oh, my. I was sure I locked it."

"Would you look at that. We didn't even think to try the knob while we were waiting," Slate said with a heavy, drawn-out Texas inflection.

Ned passed through the door and they followed. She gripped Slate's bicep, stopping before he took a step inside. Giving him a stern look, letting him know she knew what he'd done, she half mouthed, half whispered, "Hansom?"

He shrugged. "It's all that came to mind."

"Please, please. Have a seat." Ned pointed to the one chair in the room that looked like it was office furniture from the fifties. "My apologies for being late. And Mr. Hansom, there's a folding chair for you right behind the door."

"Great. Just let me scoot behind you, hon."

What game was Slate playing? Why go to such efforts to make Victor's attorney think they were a couple?

He placed the chair directly next to hers and took her hand between his, continually patting it as if comforting her. As much as she enjoyed being touched, his constant tapping reminded her of all that he had at stake. Why would he risk everything for her and Victor?

"Now that we're all settled, what can I do for you?"

"We've come about the study my—"

"Mr. Stevens, I sure hope you don't mind my being here," Slate interrupted. "Our Vivian here needed to let you know about how to contact her now. You see, her apartment caught fire last night and she lost everything she owned."

"I'm so sorry to hear that." Ned handed them a notepad and pen. "Just write your phone number down and I'll put it in your brother's file. But really, you could have just phoned. Your message mentioned something regarding a payment?"

Slate wrote two numbers and handed it back to the

attorney. Ned shuffled through several files on the corner of his desk and tugged Victor's out of the stack. He slipped the paper inside and left the folder on top.

"I thought it would be better to come down and meet you personally and let you know Vivian's not in this alone any longer. She's staying with me now."

"That's all well and good, Mr. Hansom. But I can only share details of Victor's case with Victor. I've been over this with Miss Watts several times. Her brother has been very clear about his wishes."

"He's my only family and we think we have a new le—"

"Honey, I'm sure Mr. Stevens is doing his best."

Vivian was about to let Slate *Hansom* have every pent-up frustration she'd been keeping to herself. But he smiled—a terrible fake attempt that made her want to cry.

"Look," Ned began. "There's really nothing new. You can look up the arraignment information since it's a matter of public record. The prosecutor hasn't contacted me since the first offer of a plea bargain. You know that your brother confessed but decided to go to trial. Nothing's different. If you'll excuse me, I have a very busy afternoon."

Ned Stevens, attorney at law, was only interested if more money was involved. That was very clear as he dismissed them.

"There is just one more thing, Mr. Stevens." Slate leaned forward slightly, lowering his voice. "Vivian mentioned that you've been recommending private investigators for her to work with. I hope that my humble investigation isn't going to turn up anything untoward between you and them. Is that a possibility?"

The attorney's face contorted. "Out. I'm not going to stand for you insulting me in my own office."

"You're right, Stevens." Slate's voice was back to his normal, commanding self. "Time to go, Viv."

Her stare went from man to man. Slate hadn't mentioned any of that to her. Nothing. Stevens continued to point toward his door as Hansom put the folding chair away. She managed to hold her peace until they rounded the corner by the elevators.

"I have no idea what that was all about or what it accomplished. But a heads-up would have been nice."

"Oh, man, I think I dropped my keys in the office. Be right back." He pivoted and ran back the way they'd come.

She waited at the elevator, literally tapping her foot with her arms crossed hugging her body. Right until another person walked up and pushed the down button. Vivian stepped to the other side of the hallway, concentrating on not acting annoyed. She wasn't. She was worried.

Helping her was one thing. Risking his career was quite another. What was Slate's motivation? Why would he do something like that?

"Let's go." Slate jangled his keys in the air just as the doors opened.

"Why did you keep interrupting me before I could tell him anything?"

He ignored her. He took her hand in his, holding onto her through the parking garage until he opened the door, waiting to help her into his ginormous truck. Once in her seat, he winked at her and made his clicking sound again.

"I got it."

"I know. You showed me your keys on the fifth floor."

He took several folded pieces of paper from behind his back. "No. I got your brother's file."

Chapter Fourteen

"You stole that?" Vivian's voice echoed throughout the parking garage, followed by a cough.

No one was around on their floor of the parking garage, but Slate didn't want to take any chances. He closed the passenger door then rushed inside the extended truck cab and closed his door to let her shout if she wanted.

"You okay?" He shoved a bottle of water into her hands to help with the coughing left over from the smoke inhalation.

She nodded slowly as she sipped from the bottle.

"Keep your voice down. And no, I didn't steal it." Slate scratched just above his ear, deciding he should be totally truthful. "I did sort of coerce it. If you want to get technical."

"Why?"

He'd expected her to ask how. Not why.

"Why keep your voice down? It's sort of obvious." Her look of puzzlement threw him for a loop. "Wait, why what?"

"I can't believe you'd do something so stupid." She

shook her head and rubbed her hands together the way he'd observed loved ones who worried about men he was tracking for arrest. "Why would you do something like that?"

Her anger was baffling. He'd obtained the information they both needed to continue the investigation, so why wasn't she happy?

"You're angry."

"Yes."

"At me? I'm trying to help."

"By blackmailing my brother's attorney?" Vivian's voice first raised, then dropped off to a whisper.

"That guy is definite appeals grounds for incompetency."

"You're serious? You blackmailed him."

That tone was...astonished? Was she as surprised by his actions as he was by her reaction? He hadn't explained his actions in a very long time, probably not since high school. But he could...if it would clear the air and get them out of a parking garage.

"Blackmail is too strong a word."

"It won't help Victor if you break the law and end up in jail, too."

"Wait a minute. I just sort of twisted Stevens's arm a little. I got a heads-up from Wade this morning that your lawyer friend might not be a hundred percent on the up-and-up. So I fast-forwarded the process a little by suggesting you might not press charges."

"Another decision that you made unilaterally instead of saying two words of warning to me?" She swished her curling hair from her face and behind her ear. "What if I want to sue him for the money he's taken?"

"I didn't say anything about my office not pressing charges." He grinned, hoping it would put her at ease. "Bottom line, Vivian. I'm a trained investigator. I want to investigate, to find justice for the innocent. Your brother's case reminded me of that. I just want to help."

"You really believe he's innocent? Even after the police got a full confession?"

"Things don't add up. One glance at the file and I'm wondering why no one checked out who Subject Nineteen is. I agree that person is the likely murderer. I just don't think it's your brother."

"That's your true motivation for helping us?"

"A long time ago, I decided that being a part of putting the bad guys behind bars was important. At the time, it seemed like one of the most significant things a man could do. I don't know where I got that idea. It doesn't matter. But it stuck."

"You can't become one of those men while trying to help me."

"You mean picking the lock." He cringed inside and out. "Okay, I might have been showing off a little. What if I agree to rein it in, do everything by the book? You okay with using this information?"

He lifted the papers from the seat between them. She nodded.

"Where do we start?" she asked.

"We'll need to go back to the VA Hospital. But I think checking out the information you uncovered yesterday might help us narrow down our search."

"Because someone tried to kill me?"

He put the truck in gear. "After you discovered something. Must be important."

"I'm not certain I found anything at all."

"That's where having this list is vital. We begin a search of violent crimes like you did and then compare it to the people on this list. I'll also get an appointment with the person in charge of any studies at the VA that Dr. Roberts was involved with."

At a red light, he snapped a picture of the list with his phone, stared at the image to make certain it was readable, then texted it to Heath. He turned south toward the VA Hospital on Lamar.

Vivian looked at the list. "There are at least seventy names here. It'll take quite a while to get through them."

"Not for a computer geek who knows what he's doing."

His phone rang. "Right on cue." Knowing how his partner was going to react, he lifted it to his ear instead of leaving it on speaker. "Thompson."

"No," Heath answered as predicted. "You aren't involving me in this off-books investigation that Wade instigated. I have Skylar Dawn on Saturday and told Sophie I'd cover the kid's riding lessons this weekend."

"Mom and Dad appreciate that. Since you can't help me, could you just explain how to run one of the cross searches you do?" He watched the confused looks pass across Vivian's lovely face.

"Have you asked one of the techs at headquarters?"

"Not really, but I thought I could put it together. If you walk me through it." As soon as he admitted that, he knew Hearth would know he'd been right to assume it was about Victor's case.

"Weak strategy. It won't work on me."

"What? I have a strategy? I just want your advice," Slate said, knowing his friend would see straight through his helpless act.

"No way. I'm not getting involved." Heath cut the connection.

Slate wasn't worried. Heath was reluctant…a lot. He dropped the phone in the cup holder.

"What now?" Vivian asked.

"We wait. He's going to change his mind."

"Slate, we can go to the library and look up the information ourselves. Most of it is public."

"It'll take too long. Be too public."

"But we won't be asking your friend to do something he feels uncomfortable—"

The phone rang. This time, Slate put it on speaker for her to hear.

"Fax me the originals. I'm not wasting my time typing in all these names."

"Thanks, man."

"Slate, take me off speaker."

Vivian faced the window, giving him as much privacy as a person could in the cab of a truck.

"Yeah?"

"You sure you want to do this?" Heath asked. "I'm assuming you don't want anyone around here to know what you're up to."

Slate heard office sounds in the background. "Officially, you're right. I'm not on a case. But I have less than a week to prove this theory. Their lawyer's a joke, man. He's getting kickbacks from investigators that have taken every penny she has."

"So this is charity."

"Not on your life. It's doing the right thing. Victor Watts is innocent."

"You think. I'm staring at a copy of his signed confession."

"Something's off with this one, Heath. Wade got a feeling and the same day I start looking into things, Vivian's apartment is set on fire. There may be other victims here. We gotta get to the bottom of this."

"Yeah, I know. We can only keep this under wraps so long. Somebody's going to find out what you're doing."

"I'll owe you, Heath."

There was a long pause. Long enough for Slate to drive half a block. "I'm the one who owes you, man. We both know that you're losing money boarding my horses and me until I get on my feet."

"We can get into who owes who later. I'm finding someplace to fax you this list. We need to know if anyone has been involved in a criminal outburst or worse."

"You got it."

They disconnected and Slate passed the phone to Vivian. "Can you look up a store that sends faxes?"

She did. She brought up the map so he could follow them. And then she rested her elbow on the armrest, covering her mouth with her slender hand.

Having someone be angry because he helped was new to Slate. Most of the time, he didn't care if he got credit for a win or not. Team effort and all that. But in this situation, he thought Vivian would at least be appreciative of his innovation to get Heath to help them. It was going to save tons of time.

He pressed his lips together, staring at her during the red lights. She stayed in the car when he sent the fax. He didn't get it. Shouldn't she be happy he was helping her, getting things moving along?

"What's the matter now?" he asked.

"I'm just…sort of overwhelmed. Why are you…? Whatever we do to clear my brother's name, I don't want you or your friends to get in trouble. You don't even know us."

"Vivian. Maybe I didn't explain this well before. As a Texas Ranger, I help people all the time that I don't know. You've reminded me why I got into law enforcement. To protect the innocent. I believe your brother is one of those innocents. Something happened and he needs help. I'm willing to give it."

Slate put the truck in gear and pointed it toward the VA. They'd nose around, ask if anyone had noticed anything about the man who attacked people in the cafeteria. There were lots of things they could do before getting Heath's search results.

"I can never repay you for this." Vivian used the bottom edge of her shirt to dab at tears.

"Who said I was charging?"

Chapter Fifteen

They were back.

What are they doing here? Abby had broken her routine this morning to watch the news. She knew no one had been injured in the fire. She was disappointed, but the plan wasn't perfect. It should have scared Vivian Watts or at least deterred her.

And yet, here she was, walking next to the man with a badge. They weren't on the fifth floor, where the EEG lab was located. She passed them by Admissions when she delivered paperwork to the billing office. There was no recognition on their part. They seemed to have no idea who she was.

The impulse to tear off her gloves was so overwhelming it forced her to stop in a restroom. Her cuticles needed to be cleaned but she didn't have her supplies. She picked at the edges until the perfect version of herself calmly told her to stop.

"There is no reason to panic, Abby. They don't know who you are. If they connect Rashid to you, it will only be through the EEG lab, so there's no reason to panic."

Perfectly stated and logical. They didn't know her. If

the opportunity presented itself, she could pretend, or why not initiate the introduction? She dried her hands, thinking of possibilities. Who was on her list of afternoon appointments?

"I know it will be hard, Abby, but check if the next sleep patient is here. Begin early. You can allow yourself to be ahead of schedule and let that patient follow Vivian Watts and her law enforcement officer," the voice in the mirror said.

Drawing on her protective gloves, Abby mentally prepared herself for the rigors of deviating from her routine. She needed a name for the man accompanying Victor's sister.

She could do anything if it kept her studies on track. By eliminating all the other possibilities, she'd be left with the right choice. They would obtain the perfect death. Nothing would detour them.

Abby headed to the cafeteria looking for her adversaries, for the only two people who could cause her problems. The man was easy to find. His badge was prominently displayed as he spoke to employees who worked in the cafeteria.

Vivian stood at his side. She may have looked uninterested to people who had no stake in the questioning. But Abby could see her taking notes on her smartphone. The woman was very astute.

Abby stood in line with no intention of consuming anything she bought, but she had to look inconspicuous. She had to appear to accidentally overhear the questions the man was asking. She had to obtain the introduction.

Looking on her phone, she took pictures of Victor's sister and her accomplice. *Texas Ranger Slate Thompson.*

"Excuse me," she said after a few minutes near them. "I couldn't help but overhear that you're asking about Rashid Parker. I can't believe what happened yesterday. And to think he was in the EEG lab. I just can't believe it."

Abby imitated the worry, stress and astonishment that many of the people who'd seen Rashid the previous day had demonstrated. She concentrated on the expressions the others had shown or she covered her mouth with her hand to hide her lack of emotion.

"Slate Thompson and this is Vivian Watts."

"Abby Norman. I assist the EEG lab technician." She pulled her hands back to her sides before the ranger reached out to touch her. "He was such a nice man."

"Can you tell us what an EEG lab is and what you do there?" Vivian asked.

"An electroencephalogram is a test that detects electrical activity in your brain. I help set it up for the technician, type up notes, get the patients settled. I have no idea why any of them need monitoring. You'd have to ask their doctors."

"Thanks. You've been very helpful," Slate said, then turned back to Vivian.

How dare he be so dismissive!

"Walk away," said the voice from the mirror. "You know who they are. Now you can eliminate them both."

Chapter Sixteen

After getting a handle on Rashid Parker's day, they hadn't discovered anything that would have set off a rampage. Vivian didn't feel any closer to discovering why her brother had been accused of murder. Heath had narrowed down the list of names from the sleep study. Names, numbers and addresses were now being compared to crime reports.

"You look discouraged," Slate said.

"Four hours in that hospital and, yes, I feel useless. Are we making any headway?"

"We have a list of names to check out. We also know that Parker just seemed to lose it over nothing. The guy was eating lasagna and salad one minute and stabbing someone the next. Other than that, no one can remember anything unusual about him. We know he wasn't angry, wasn't complaining, wasn't talking to himself, wasn't unusual in any outward way."

"What does any of that tell us?"

"It sort of fits the description of your brother. No outward signs of distress. Parker seems to have just snapped."

"You said several names on this list had committed violent crimes?"

"Yes."

"Another reason to interview their family and friends."

Vivian walked closely at Slate's side. She was skimming the list on his phone, trying to find the names she'd discovered last night. They had parked in the hospital's farthest southern lot, one of the newest overflow areas that still had construction machinery in the corner. It was away from the main buildings and garage cameras.

They were almost back to the truck when she heard a loud wail. A different type of dread took over her body. Fright of the unknown, but with the feeling of an attack.

Slate pushed her aside. She fell on her knees onto a median of newly planted grass. She heard running footsteps as the scream of attack got closer. Out of the corner of her eye, she saw a large man hit Slate across his shoulders with something.

She rolled to her back, looking for the phone. Getting help was all she could think of to do. Their attacker lifted a piece of wood to hit Slate again.

"Hey!"

He had a wild, crazy look in his dark eyes. Longish hair, a green jacket with patches. She didn't know how she focused on so much of him, but she took it all in. Army boots like her brother wore.

The shout came from her. She crab-walked backward on the grass to get away when the man faced her. But before he took two steps, Slate was on his feet, jerking the man's arm to spin him around.

Slate looked like a man who was used to dealing with attackers. Each move seemed automatic, ready for the anticipated blow. Maybe in a normal fight, the other man wouldn't have stood a chance. But the attacker looked like he was on drugs.

Wild-eyed and crazed. Slow but hard, deliberate movements. A car pulled through the drive, distracting the attacker. Spinning, Slate lifted his leg and let the force of his boot knock the crazy man's piece of wood behind a backhoe.

Slate shoved a shoulder into the man's middle. They both went down into a pile of construction rubble.

Their attacker grabbed a piece of loose rebar and charged. Slate blocked the crazy man's swing, keeping the rebar inches away from his skull. They went down a second time.

Rolling over. Then back. Slate punched the man's side until he cringed, giving Slate the split second he needed to throw him off and roll to a crouch. This time, the man shook his head, looked around, turned and ran.

By the time Slate was on his feet and running, a car sped out of the parking garage. Vivian couldn't catch any of the license plate. Her eyes locked with the surprised look on the man's face as he drove away.

This man might have answers to their questions. She ran after the car, but he turned the corner and was gone. Slate caught up with her and pulled her to a stop, swinging her around into his arms.

"You okay?"

She nodded and looked at the crowd gathering at the doctor's entrance. Men were approaching, others pointing.

"Get in the truck," Slate ordered. "Quick."

"We're not waiting on the police? Do you think we can catch him ourselves?"

"No. He's gone. I'd prefer to go home and not hang around to talk with the VA or DPD."

"Aren't we going to check out these names?"

"We're going home."

"But what if—"

"Dammit, Vivian. You may not need to regroup, but I just took a two-by-four across my shoulders. My jaw hurts like a slab of concrete hit it. Oh, wait—it did. I need an ice pack, aspirin and a shower."

BACK AT HIS HOUSE, Slate didn't waste any time before putting three aspirin into his palm, swallowing them and jumping into the shower. He was sore but with no permanent damage. The forty-minute ride back from the hospital had been pretty quiet. Vivian plugged in his phone for power and searched through the list.

He didn't mind. His head was full of questions. Had their attacker been hypnotized? Drugged?

The first thing that was clear to him was that he'd never seen the man who'd attacked them before. The second thing was that the man had been intent on doing serious damage, not robbing them.

Coincidence?

How many times had he hated that word? When he was working a case, it just didn't feel right as an explanation. There was only one logical answer. Someone in the hospital was related to the murder of Dr. Roberts and the suicide of Rashid Parker.

But how?

What did one have to do with the other?

The quick shower he took did nothing for the soreness between his shoulder blades. And nothing to answer the many questions he'd racked up on the drive home.

The steam of the shower in the small bathroom didn't cover the smell of his mother's fajitas from the other room. Spicy chicken and beef, fresh salsa and warm tortillas… His stomach growled while he dressed and listened to laughter in the kitchen.

"Okay, I hear Slate. I better skedaddle." His father gave him a thumbs-up before he pulled the front door shut behind him.

"Feel better?" Vivian asked.

"Cleaner at least." Slate gestured to the closed plastic containers. "You eat?"

"I was waiting on you. It smells delicious."

"Mom's a great cook. She still hasn't passed on her special marinating recipe. Hungry?"

"Starved. I think we skipped lunch."

"My stomach doesn't have to think about that. It knows the answer."

Vivian was dressed the same but seemed more relaxed. Had his dad accomplished something in the last ten minutes that Slate hadn't been able to do by being with her all day?

He passed her a plate and pulled lids off the containers. His mother had gone all out. He recognized the homemade guacamole and knew how good it would be. What he didn't know was if his parents really understood that Vivian wasn't a girlfriend.

They dug into the food.

"This is really delicious." She took another bite, then another. "So what do we do next? I have some names and—"

"Eat. We eat. I'll grab my laptop after and see what Heath recommends."

"Oh," she said, swallowing a bite. "I didn't mean to read the texts, but you gave me your phone to work on and they kept popping up."

He finished off his first fajita and made a second while he waited on Vivian to barely touch hers. He stretched his arms, then rolled his neck trying to relieve the tenseness.

"You have a road rash." She set her plate aside and retrieved his cold pack from the freezer, wrapping it in a dish towel before holding it against the side of his face.

He winced, pulling away. She gently cupped his chin to keep him from moving.

"It didn't look as bad as that makes it feel," he mumbled out of the corner of his mouth that he could move. "Thanks, by the way."

He replaced her hand with his to hold the cold pack against the scrape. "I'm the one who should be thanking you. One word and you turned that guy's attention away from splitting my head in two."

"Then you kept him away from me. I don't understand the why of it all. Do you think he was the one who set the apartment fire last night?" She sat and picked up her fajita.

"I don't know. I was too slow to catch any of the plate number."

"Me either. Do you think he's on this list?"

"I don't know what's connecting all this together. It just keeps getting stranger. Eat up. It's better hot."

They ate and each downed a bottle of water. He wiped his lips and rolled his neck again, making a note that a chiropractor visit may be in his future.

"Do you need to see a doctor?" Vivian asked.

"Not yet. Hey, what did Heath say in that text?"

"That he was called to a scene and not to expect him home."

He snapped the plastic lids back onto their containers. Before he could stand, she already had them stacked and in the refrigerator.

"Do you think it would hurt you if I rubbed your neck a little? I don't want to make it worse," she said while washing up their dishes.

"Go for it."

She rubbed her hands together to warm them. He didn't care when they were still cool against his skin. She kneaded around the neck of his T-shirt, then across to the top of his shoulders.

"That feel okay? Nothing seems out of place."

"No. Just sore. I feel stupid that I let someone run up behind us with a two-by-four."

"We've had a long day. There's nothing to feel bad about."

"I am running on a couple of hours of sleep. I haven't

done that in a while now. Most of my job lately has been eight to six."

"That explains it then."

He felt some of the stiffness melting away. It was a little sensitive where the board had hit, maybe bruised, but with each squeeze and knead of the muscle, it relaxed.

"It's a lot better. Thanks."

"Would you mind if I used your laptop? I could sign on as a guest if you have anything I shouldn't see."

"Sure, and it's totally my personal files. Mainly ranch inventory, stuff like that. I don't bring office files home for my laptop." They moved the short distance to the living room, giving him time to realize she *was* the work-related file that he'd brought home. "I'll go get it."

He grabbed the laptop from his dresser and hobbled back to Vivian just in time to catch her rubbing her own neck.

"Did you get hurt when you fell?"

"No. It's just normal stiffness from sleeping on a couch and working as a waitress."

He set the laptop on the coffee table and walked behind the couch, which sat in the middle of the room, separating it from the kitchen. He could easily reach Vivian's shoulders from there.

"Sit back. Let me return the favor. I got this."

At least, he thought he did. Right up to the moment he touched her curly hair and dropped it to her left shoulder. Right up to the time he touched the tense tendons across her back. Maybe right up to the moment he saw his fingertips dip under the edge of her shirt.

Or it might have been the exact moment he realized Heath wouldn't be coming home.

Chapter Seventeen

Slate's right fingertips skimmed the supersensitive part of her neck that curved into her shoulder. His left fingers joined in on the opposite side before all ten gently but firmly massaged.

For the first minute, Vivian couldn't really think. It had been so long since she'd had the muscles in her neck artfully manipulated. Strong fingers hit a knot and immediately began to untangle it.

"How's that? Too much?"

"No," she said, keeping it simple. If she didn't, she'd be blathering about how absolutely wonderful it felt.

He pushed his hands under the loose neck of the T-shirt and kneaded the tops of her shoulders. He never broke contact with her skin, just kept kneading and stroking.

"You're really good. Have you had lessons about how…to do this?" Her eyes had closed somewhere after the first minute or two.

"Nothing professional."

"Should you be doing this?"

"I'll stop if you want me to." His hands paused. She shrugged and he began kneading her shoulder blade.

Why have him stop? This was innocent enough. Just a shoulder rub. Nothing unprofessional. No. Wait. Everything about it was unprofessional, but was there anything about their relationship that should remain segregated? Hadn't they already crossed a line since she was staying at his house?

If she were honest, she'd wanted to cross a line when she'd first seen him sitting in her booth at the wings restaurant. The desire grew with everything they did together.

"I hope you don't expect one of these in return. You're turning me into mush."

"Good. You need a little relaxing."

"I admit that eleven months of sleeping on that lumpy pullout called a mattress has done horrible things to my muscles."

"I can tell." Slate shook her shoulders a little to emphasize his words. "Come on, relax a little. You know you're safe here."

Yes, she was safe. But it was still hard to let go of the stress caused by trying to free her brother. Stress and the guilt of being free when he wasn't.

"There you go again. Tensing up. Stop thinking about it." His strong fingers slid confidently across the loose shirt and the flesh underneath. "None of this is your fault. No matter how much you try to take the blame."

"For someone who wants me to forget about Victor, you sure are saying a lot to remind me."

"True."

Slate's fingers stopped kneading. She heard his booted footsteps leave his place behind the couch and go into the kitchen. Listened to the fridge open, to a glass clink.

Okay, so relaxation was over. She closed her eyes and tried to stop her brain. Stop it from racing down the path of helping her brother. That wasn't completely true. Her pulse was racing because of Slate's touch. Because she wanted more than a shoulder rub.

She desired the human contact he provided. Shoot... she desired him. Back in Miami, she might have already invited him to dinner at her apartment. She might have slid her hands around his neck and suggested a long good-night kiss.

It was comical how much she wanted to just *be* with him.

Actually, there wasn't anything funny about her desire. All he had to do was sit next to her in his truck and her body trembled.

Aching for him was the easy part. Would there be a future? Did she have the right to think about what came next after Victor's trial?

"You're thinking about the case again." Slate offered her a beer.

"How can you tell?"

"You crinkle your forehead and flatten your lips." He gestured for her to scoot to the middle of the couch.

She moved, then took a sip of the ice-cold ale. "That look doesn't sound very pretty at all."

"On the contrary. I have a sister. I can imagine what you've been going through. I don't think I could put it on the back burner either." He turned to where his back was against the arm of the couch. "Come here."

She was surprised, but then again, she wasn't. She stood so one of his legs could stretch the length of the cushions, then she sat between his legs, resting against his chest.

They sipped their beers in silence.

Slate's free hand played with her hair, curling it around his finger.

The curtains blew away from the wide windowsill, cracked open to cool the sunshine that had been pouring into the living room. No one was around. Slate's parents were at the main house. Heath was at Company B headquarters.

Horses whinnied and the breeze blew through the trees. Other than something buzzing against the glass panes, there wasn't any noise. Very different from the low-income apartments where she'd heard every word of her neighbors. And very different from the apartment she'd had in Miami with the high-end stereo that drowned out every plane or argument.

Slate's fingers outlined the top of her ear, then the edges, drawing circles across her skin. She stopped thinking, concentrating on the early evening light shining on the hardwood floor. Once or twice, his finger swept across her forehead, checking on her tension. He softly smoothed her hair, again and again.

The next moment her eyes opened to a cooler and darker room. She must have relaxed. Completely.

The sun was setting, and brilliant colors beckoned them to watch through the front window. She could feel Slate behind her, awake. But he remained silent as they watched the shadows grow deeper.

The bottles had been set on the coffee table. Hers half-full, his empty. She began to sit forward when Slate's fingers lifted her long hair, draping it over her left shoulder. His fingers tapped across her shoulders before dancing down her spine, sending splendid shivers through her body.

His mouth grazed the side of her neck. Her head fell back, again resting on his chest, rolling to the left and giving him more access. As his light and teasing lips caressed her skin, he skimmed her shoulder with his knuckles before sliding his hands over the top of her arms.

Slate got up, laced the fingers of one hand with Vivian's, helped her to her feet and somehow twirled her straight into his arms. Their eyes connected and she was lost.

The first brush of his lips touched the corner of her mouth. A little hesitant. Was he trying to decide whether to continue or if she would reject him? She didn't dwell on the question, instead answered for herself. She turned her face slightly so their mouths lined up completely and pressed her lips to his.

The clean smell of his skin mixed with the smokiness of the fajitas. His breath was hot and created more wanton desire within her.

Each time their lips touched, the need inside her grabbed hold and wouldn't let go. It was anchored to something she didn't understand because nothing had ever reached that part of her before.

It scared her enough to run, yet spurred her forward at the same time. She tried to retreat and Slate deepened their kiss. His mouth was a warm haven, a taste that belonged only to him.

They'd been close to moving forward with the case and now they were closer to falling onto his bed. But she wasn't a fool. She could back away, douse this dynamite before it was ever ignited. They were still wearing all their clothes. All she had to do was take a step back.

He'd behave.

Just place her hand on his chest and step away from the only man who was helping her for all the right reasons. She'd be the only one to know what she passed up. No one would ever know how afraid she'd been to get involved.

She hadn't been close to anyone since moving to Texas, longer still because she'd been focusing on a career or in the army. What did one night making love with a man she actually respected matter?

All she had to do was say no.

Warning bells went off. Sirens louder than the fire trucks the night before.

She didn't want it to stop, but she forced the words that would keep their relationship at the same level.

"I should probably go to bed."

"Too early," Slate whispered, kissing her collarbone.

God, he was good at that.

"I'm not…I'm not really sure if we should be doing this."

He tugged her shirt down her arm, baring her shoulder more, and scraped his teeth across. Those luscious shivers that started in her core and traveled to every nerve ending encompassed her again.

"Do you think this is too dangerous?"

"Pretty much, yes." Her breathy words barely registered.

"It can't be as dangerous as a man trying to kill you."

Oh, I think I'm dying a little bit right now.

Vivian pressed her body closer. The cute borrowed top she wore was quickly tugged loose from her jeans. His was already free.

His calloused fingers smoothed the hot skin of her back. Hers explored the toned, muscular, sculpted man who had saved her. It would take very little maneuvering to shrug out of their clothes and into each other.

Imagining how she'd feel the morning after didn't compare to actually having his lips against hers, having his tongue tease in an age-old dance. Nothing was rational. She wanted to *feel*. Not think of consequences, threats or reality.

"How am I supposed to resist you?" she asked. Threats of fire and men swinging boards got pushed to the back of her mind when she timidly guided his hand to her breast.

"You want to?" he asked, his lips whispering on top of her own.

She answered with another kiss. No longer afraid of possible consequences or conflicts. He was man. She was woman.

The intensity of their kisses grew. They tugged each other out of their shirts. They steadied each other as they shimmied out of their pants. Maybe it shouldn't happen, but it was happening. They explored each other's bodies with their hands and eyes.

Magnificent. A word she completely understood now. Slate dropped to his knees, exploring further.

"I have an idea." Vivian heard her hoarse voice squeak the words when his thumbs hooked inside the edge of her skimpy underwear.

"I have one, too," he answered with an inviting smile. He turned her body until it relaxed on the couch.

Vivian's idea evaporated in the heat generated from Slate's caresses.

Chapter Eighteen

The adrenaline rush during the fight had kept him going through his shower. He'd begun to relax and slow down a little during the neck rub Vivian had given him. Then he'd touched her silky skin.

The rush was back and touching her wasn't enough.

He wanted all of her. Mind, body… Yeah, everything.

Slate swallowed hard at the realization of how much he was attached to Vivian. He'd known her two days and she was a huge part of his thoughts. He backed away, pushing the coffee table toward the television.

The look on his face had to be confusing her. She was squinting, asking what was wrong without any words.

"Nothing."

The corners of Vivian's mouth rose in a smile. First one side, then the other, along with a nicely shaped eyebrow.

"What color are your eyes?" he asked.

They looked smoky, sort of a grayish blue.

"What?" She seemed surprised and pushed the left

strap of her bra onto her upper arm. "Probably gray. They change color."

"I thought they were different yesterday." He took a finger and lifted the right strap off her delicate shoulder to let it drape on her arm.

He stood, stretching his hands toward her. She took them and he helped her stand. He led her around the couch, walking backward. His imagination was in overdrive but he moved slowly.

Vivian's expression changed more rapidly than his sex-seeking mind could keep up. Anticipation to quizzical to embarrassment—all in the time it took to move a step away from her. She dropped her hands, crossing her arms over her breasts.

"Someone's out there."

He spun around. It had to be Heath. No one else would be coming to the house. His parents would have called, not walked over.

"One of the horses—"

"A horse doesn't have a short beard."

Slate spun to face the front of the house. "Like the guy from—"

The door burst in, bouncing off the cabinet of DVDs. Vivian screamed in surprise.

"Get to the bathroom," Slate yelled.

She'd be safe there. But she didn't run. She only backed up.

His weapon was in the lockbox. His phone on the dining table. His shoes weren't on his feet. Hell, he wasn't even wearing pants.

"What do you want?" Slate asked him.

The man from the hospital was wide-eyed and crazy looking. He moved from side to side, almost indecisive about what to do next. The baseball bat in his hand slammed against the open door. Then slammed again, leaving a good-sized hole.

"Look, man. If I did something to offend you, let's talk. I'm sure we can work this out."

"Slate? Can he hear you?" Vivian asked, her hands on top of his shoulders.

"Not sure." He shrugged her hands away, preparing to defend himself. He lowered his voice to a whisper, "I need you to get to the bedroom or bath, Vivian. I'll do better if all I have to defend is myself."

"Can you get him into the living room corner? I could get to your phone and call 911."

"No. It'll take too long for them to get here."

"All right. I'll get out of your way then."

Slate took her at her word. With no idea why the guy was waiting to attack, he stepped onto the couch, ready to jump behind it and lure him away from Vivian. He waved his hand behind his back, indicating to her to join him, run and get to safety.

She raised a foot onto a couch cushion and the man grunted. Grunted like a cave man.

"What's with this guy?" Slate wondered aloud.

Vivian ignored him and moved in the opposite direction—she'd be trapped in the corner. The man turned the same way. She moved closer to the TV, dipping to the coffee table and grabbing Slate's shirt.

"Do you know him?" Slate asked.

"No," Vivian whispered. "Why doesn't he do something?"

"Can you keep his attention on you?" Slate waited for her to take another step away from him, then jumped lightly over the top of the couch to the floor.

The man blinked slowly but kept his gaze glued to Vivian. He grunted again. She took a step back. He advanced, swinging the bat.

Slate had one chance. He shoved off the end of the hall wall and tackled the man before he got too far into the room. Or too close to Vivian. The bat stayed locked in his hand.

Slate managed to stay on the man's back. The attacker flung his arm—and the bat—from side to side as he rolled, trying to get free. Things crashed, breaking around his head. Slate tried to get a choke hold on the man, but he had to let go to block the bat from connecting with his head.

Slate saw Vivian cross the room. If she got his phone before running out the door, she wouldn't be able to unlock it.

The attacker growled, jerking the bat. Slate tugged it free from both their hands. It rolled under the couch. The man used that moment to shove Slate off his back. He scrambled to his knees and followed Vivian.

A split second later, Slate pursued both across the driveway, toward the main house. "Vivian," he yelled after her. "Back door!"

She ran.

The attacker followed, yelling like a madman.

Slate ran, the stones from the driveway better than the burrs and stickers he knew to be at its edge. They all kept running.

Damn, I wish I had my weapon.

He gained on the attacker, who was gaining on Vivian. She made it to the enclosed back porch, slamming through the screen door and dropping to the other side where he couldn't see her.

Slate was a body-length away from the attacker and dove. He caught the man around the ankles, tripping him to the ground. He just had to latch on until his father plowed through the back door. The man twisted, sitting and beating on Slate's back with both hands.

"Stop!" Vivian yelled from the steps, coming closer.

"Stay back!" Slate warned.

The man was pretty strong and still acting like he was possessed. He turned. Slate dug his fingers into the man's jeans, pulling himself closer as the man tried to crawl toward Vivian.

"What the hell's going on here?"

"Dad, help me stop this guy!" Slate yelled.

His father pumped a shell into his shotgun. The sound alone should have scared a normal man. But this guy was far from normal. He kept clawing at the ground to move inches, dragging Slate.

His dad raised the gun and used the butt to hit the man on the back of the head. All movement stopped.

"You all right, son?"

Slate stood, Vivian at his elbow. His father aimed the shotgun at the intruder, who was out cold.

"Yeah, I'm good." He turned to Vivian, who had

managed to pull his shirt over her underclothes. "How 'bout you?"

"Nothing worth mentioning. Thanks for your help," she said to his dad.

"You calling the police?"

"Yeah. First we're going to tie this son of a bitch up. Mind getting some rope, Dad?" Slate held out his hand for the shotgun, which his dad passed to him.

"I'll call the cops on my way." His dad pulled out his phone and dialed as he headed to the shed next to the barn.

"You really okay?" Slate asked Vivian.

"My feet are sore. He never got a hold of me. Did you realize your knees are bleeding?"

"Slate? Everything under control now?" his mom asked from the porch.

"Yes, ma'am. We're good. Could you walk with Vivian back to my house?"

"She doesn't need to do that," Vivian whispered.

"Just let me get my shoes," his mom replied.

"Why did you ask her to do that? She's going to know what was going on. This is so embarrassing." Vivian covered her face.

"Sweetheart, I think they took one look at us and figured that out. Could you send back my jeans, boots and phone?"

The screen door swung shut and his mom dropped a blanket around Vivian's shoulders. "Come on, sugar. No need for everybody to catch their death out here. That storm last night brought in a cold front."

The women walked up the driveway. His dad returned with rope before the attacker moaned. Slate passed off the shotgun while he looped the rope and tied the guy up.

"Maybe you should hog-tie him to make him stay put," his father joked. "The local PD said they were ten minutes away. I sure am glad a Texas Ranger lives around here."

"Yeah, Heath's on an assignment."

"Where am I? What's…what's going on?" The man's voice shook, sounding confused and frightened.

Slate helped him sit up and lean against the porch, taking his wallet out of his back pocket. "So, Allan Pinkston. Why are you at my house and why did you attack me? Don't pretend to not know what's going on."

"I attacked you? I…I don't even know you. How did I get here?"

"I assume you followed us in the car you drove off in after you hit me with a two-by-four at the hospital this afternoon."

"No way, man. I don't even know who you are. Last thing I remember is being at the VA. Did you dose me or something?"

"What about Vivian Watts? You know her?"

"I've got no idea who that is. Why does my head hurt so bad?"

Slate could usually tell when a suspect was lying. Either this man was really, really good at it, or he was genuinely confused.

"You were attacked twice today, son?" his father asked.

"Yes, sir."

"By this guy?"

"Or his twin."

The stranger shook his head. "I don't have any brother and I didn't attack you. What are you going to do with me?"

"Let the cops sort it out," Slate answered. "If I were you, I'd insist on a drug test to see if someone did slip you something."

His mom returned with his pants just in time to pull on his boots before the Rockwall police arrived to take Pinkston into custody. They found a car registered to their attacker on the main road.

Sometimes being a ranger was a good thing. It limited the explanations needed to convince Rockwall PD to take a trip by the hospital to verify what Pinkston was high on before booking him.

Slate failed to mention Vivian's involvement. Pinkston didn't seem to remember anything. The charges were trespassing and assaulting a law enforcement officer. Slate needed to go by the station the next day to file a complaint.

"I hope you know what you're doing, son." His dad had his shotgun resting on his shoulder as they walked to Slate's house.

"I have to admit that this case is all over the place. Murder. A fire. An attack by a guy who seems to have amnesia. Weird."

"Yeah, weird. Mom and I will still leave tomorrow. That is, unless you need me to stay. I can watch Vivian if you need to chase a lead down or something."

Slate stopped to look at his old man. "Thanks, Dad.

But I got it covered. Leaving probably is a good idea." They clapped each other on the shoulder, then finished their walk to the house.

"I sure hope you know what you're doing, Slate," his father repeated. "I know I'm not a cop, but you might consider keeping your boots closer."

In other words, he might do a better job by keeping his pants on. Slate agreed.

Before stepping into the house with his father, Slate called the man who got him into this situation.

"Wade, I think you, me and Jack need to have a conversation. I can be there in half an hour."

Chapter Nineteen

Wade threw another ball of trash into the far corner wastebasket and yes, pretended like it was a basketball. No one watched. No one was around. The nine-to-fivers had left for the day. He still had a couple more files to get through to meet his daily goal.

The door opened, the wind whipping it all the way back as Jack arrived.

"This better be good." He looked around at the empty office. "And hopefully on the books this time."

"I should be back out there, fighting criminals or helping on one of the weirdest cases of a lifetime," he said aloud, instead of just thinking it for once.

Sick of sitting behind a desk, Wade was living vicariously through his fellow rangers. Waiting on a call or information. Wanting to be right about his hunch. Setting up meetings between Slate and Jack.

"What you need to do is keep your nose clean until the major says otherwise," Jack told him. "We can handle things. Even the weird stuff."

The door opened again. Slate escorted a woman

who must have been Vivian Watts to his desk across from Wade.

"You know I could run some of those names Heath sent you."

"No!" both Slate and Jack said together. They startled Vivian and both gave him a look like he was crazy.

"I can work the list," Jack said. "I'll be patrolling most of those neighborhoods anyway."

Obviously, Slate had already spoken to him about what needed to be done.

The outer office door burst open and Heath marched in, heavy boots on the worn linoleum. "Is my TV still in one piece?" he asked Slate, referring to the fight that had taken place in their living room.

"As a matter of fact, it's better than my head," Slate replied.

Vivian Watts sat on the edge of the conversation, obviously paying attention and purposely restraining her opinion. It was obvious since she had eyes only for her hero…Slate.

Heath gave her a strange look. Maybe he recognized the shirt she wore was one of Slate's. But what was strange about that? All her clothes were gone in a fire. And yet, Slate seemed preoccupied until Jack had mentioned the list they were waiting on from Heath. Then Slate had been quick to jump in that it had been Vivian's idea.

Dammit, Slate. You're falling for her?

"Have you found anything significant with Allan Pinkston's background check?" Jack asked.

"I guess Slate hasn't gotten to the *P*s on the sleep-study list."

"Pinkston's on it?" Slate asked. "This doesn't make sense."

"Do you think he's Subject Nineteen?" Vivian asked, turning all the men's heads toward her. Which in turn had them all looking at Slate.

"Maybe we should talk in the hall?" Jack suggested.

"Be right back, Vivian." Slate almost cooed.

"Stay." Jack looked at Wade with the direct order.

"Looks like I'm keeping you company for a while," Wade said to Vivian. "I'm Wade Hamilton and I assume you're Vivian. Guess they forgot we haven't met. You getting along with Slate okay?"

He already knew the answer. Her blush confirmed his suspicions as his fellow rangers disappeared into the hallway.

"Are they always this bossy?" Vivian remained in Slate's chair, sitting across from Wade. "So, why are you stuck here with me instead of with those three, making plans?"

"I'm supposed to have plausible deniability. They're trying to keep me out of trouble." Even though he was the one who'd started everything three weeks ago. By begging Jack to take his place and rescue Megan Harper—now Jack's girlfriend—Wade had gotten himself banged up and assigned to desk duty.

"Thank you." Vivian waved his attention back to the present. "Talking through what's happening should be helpful. I'm glad you could wait around for us."

"It's not like I have a lot to do." He patted the files

living on the corner of his desk. "I'm officially off the streets."

And officially without a life.

"So you're the one who gave Slate my brother's case, right?"

"That's me."

"I can't thank you enough for what you've done."

"I didn't do anything except ask a question."

"I know Slate wouldn't be helping me if it wasn't for you. He told me as much when we met." She stood and began pacing the short open space between the desks on the next row.

Wade leaned back in his office chair, openly admiring Vivian's shapely form. From what Heath had mentioned about Slate's interest, they were both pretty certain he would have found some reason to look into her brother's case.

"From what's happened around you in the past twenty-four hours, it's a good thing he's at your side. Slate's a good man."

She nodded in agreement and looked like she might cry. "I appreciate everything you've all done, especially Slate."

The guys came back into the office just as Vivian politely covered her mouth.

Vivian Watts had more than appreciation in her eyes. It was a look that represented something Wade could envy. The spark of love or something close to it. He'd seen it a couple of times now. Never aimed in his direction, though.

Did that mean he was ready for it? Nope.

Hey, he was a bachelor and proud of his status. The last thing he needed was a girlfriend. Or a serious relationship.

"We're out of here, man." Slate darted in the door, gathered Vivian under his arm and got out fast. "Thanks."

Heath ignored Vivian and kept walking out the door.

Jack waited for the others to leave then wandered to Wade's desk. He rapped a knuckle on the corner files. "It's another good hunch. This won't last forever. You'll be out there fighting the good fight soon enough. You should lock up and go home."

"Be cool," Wade said as the door shut behind his partner.

It was late. He should go home.

Instead, he flipped open another file, brought the number up on the computer and began the process of verification. He really should get a life. Or maybe at least go on a date. But one woman kept breezing through his thoughts, pushing all the others aside... Therese Ortiz.

Repaying the favor he owed her was the reason he sat in this chair instead of doing the work he loved. *Your pigheadedness got you stuck behind this desk. Not a woman.* He couldn't help his natural curiosity, he argued with himself. Was it his fault that he wanted to know more about her and what she did?

Therese was exciting. An unknown that he couldn't predict.

The broken ribs ached. He carefully sucked in a deep breath, expanding his lungs to capacity. Testing them. Disappointed in their reaction.

After two weeks, the swelling was gone from his eye and the bruise looked like a yellow stain on his skin. He'd tried to find out what had happened to Therese or where she'd gone after her arrest, but all records of her involvement with the Harper case had disappeared.

So had the number he'd contacted her through before.

Wade wasn't a patient man and hated to wait for Therese to reach out. But he knew without a doubt that she'd call.

And that he'd answer.

Chapter Twenty

"I want to help. I can be useful. You even told your friends that it was my idea to look up other veterans who may have had problems." Vivian had voiced all the arguments in the truck on the return drive to Slate's home.

He still hadn't told her what he, Jack and Heath had discussed in the hallway out of her earshot. In fact, he'd been very closemouthed since asking her if she was ready to leave Company B headquarters.

"Did I miss a key piece of information? Did they discover something you don't want to tell me?" she asked.

He shook his head and turned down the drive to his ranch house. It was completely dark at this end, but she could see the porch lights at both houses. There was no way to see a dark car parked along the road here. She hoped he wasn't blaming himself for Allan Pinkston's attack.

"You sure are quiet," she said.

He parked his truck, cut the engine and gripped the steering wheel so tightly she could see the blood leaving his knuckles. Whatever he was working up the courage to say wasn't going to be good.

"I have to apologize," he said.

"For what?"

"Letting my guard down like that could have cost you your life."

"I think we both let our guards down."

Somehow she knew that he'd withdraw even more if she extended her hand to touch him like she wanted. Going inside and trying to pick up where they'd left off would be awkward to say the least. Another intimate moment like that would bring up his need to apologize.

Yeah, it wouldn't work. The possibility of a relationship with this kind man had passed.

"If you could take me to the women's shelter in the morning, that would be great."

"I don't blame you for thinking... Hell, I'm totally at fault here. You lost your apartment and everything you owned. I should never have put you in a position where you thought you had to have sex with me."

"What?"

"I want you to know that you're welcome to stay here as long as it takes to get back on your feet. I spoke to my mom—"

"You think I was going to sleep with you for payment?"

He shook his head so hard the truck bounced. "No, not that. But a lot's happened you might have..."

"Go ahead. I dare you to say that I'm a poor little ol' female. So totally confused and overwhelmed by my situation that I'd sleep with the only *man* who extended me a kind word. Go ahead."

"That's not what I meant at all."

"You know, Slate, *you* approached *me*. I didn't ask for your help." She jumped down from the truck, slamming the door. She marched several steps before she realized she had nothing to collect from inside.

She really did own nothing, and her smoky suitcase was still in the back of the truck. She pivoted with her next step and saw Slate still inside the truck cab, mouth open, probably wondering what had just happened.

She got back inside. "I'm not staying with you more than it takes to drive me someplace I can stay tonight or drop me under a bridge with a cardboard box."

It was Slate who reached out and rubbed her shoulder. "I'm sorry."

"I'm serious."

"I know you are. I spoke with my parents before we left. We can sleep in the main house."

"No."

He pulled the keys from the ignition and shoved them into his pocket. "It's nonnegotiable. Heath and Jack agreed that it's too dangerous to stay here. Whoever's after you knows where I live."

"That means it's too risky to stay with your parents."

"My parents are leaving in the morning. The alternative is us in the same room at a motel." He shoved his hands through his short hair. "I know that's not a good idea. It makes better sense to be somewhere with more than one room."

"Just take me to a shelter."

He shifted, winced at the muscle strain and stretched his neck. She would offer to rub the kinks out again, but that's how this all started, with an innocent gesture.

"Look." He dropped his hand on top of her shoulder again. "If you insist on going somewhere… I get it. There's a motel back on Interstate 30, I'll get a room. You can take the bed and I'll camp out in front of the door. But I'd feel safer here with Dad's shotgun pointed out the window while I catch some shut-eye."

She'd forgotten that he hadn't slept much. For that matter, neither had she.

"We are already here. Is there something I could do? Like keep watch? I've done it before in the military. Or maybe some chores? I'd love to repay you and your family." Was she giving in and accepting his charity because she didn't want to find a way to repay him for a hotel room? Was her mind actually working that way now?

Did it matter? She had few choices. Humbling herself to keep the rangers working on Victor's case hadn't been as difficult as before she'd kissed Slate.

"That's not necessary."

"My only goal at the moment is to get my brother out of jail. I'll worry about my life and Victor's after he's free and clear of these charges. So I need to accept your charity for now."

"That's not what I had in mind when I apologized."

"No apology necessary." She meant it. Whether it sounded sincere or not wasn't something she could correct at the moment. "I guess I should get the things you bought me together and move to your parents' spare bedroom?"

"That's probably best."

The gravel crunched under their feet as they got

out of the truck and went to the porch. So much had changed since they'd made the short walk earlier that evening before dinner. Even after the attack at the hospital, she'd felt lighthearted and good for the first time in months. Now…not so much.

"Care to share what you guys talked about without me?" she asked once inside.

"A game plan of sorts." He went to the closet and got a gym bag, smelling the inside before handing it to her. "We split up the list. I didn't mean to segregate you."

"Oh, I realize that. Wade explained it was him you were trying to protect." That still made it sound like she was upset about being excluded. "I'm not angry or anything. Just curious what the plans are for tomorrow. When I should wake up, et cetera."

"Well…"

"Oh, no. I'm not waiting here with your horses while you discover who set up my brother. Please don't strand me here to wait."

"I told Jack you wouldn't go for it." He moved stiffly, attempting not to bend his knee.

"What's wrong?" She pointed to his legs.

"Just need a couple of bandages across my knees from when I fell earlier. I think the blood dried to my pants."

She was going to regret her next words. "Drop your jeans and let me see." Just stay angry, and they'd be safe.

"Nothing doing. That is *not* a good idea."

Vivian placed her hands on her hips for emphasis. "Do you honestly think I'd sleep with you after you practically called me a prostitute?"

"I didn't say anything like that. You've been through a lot of trauma whether you recognize it or not."

"Is that what your buddies at Company B told you?" She took a step closer to him and reached for his rodeo belt buckle to force him to comply.

He tried to jump back but stiffened in pain.

"Come on, Slate. You need help and I'm here. We are not going to sleep together. Ever. Not now. And it's not like I haven't see your plaid boxers before." She walked toward his bathroom. "Where are the bandages and peroxide? In here?"

"There's a first aid kit on the top shelf of the laundry cabinet."

She heard the sound of a large belt buckle hitting the floor along with a couple of curses. "I'm not taking my boots off and making it easy to undress."

"Suit yourself."

Finding the first aid kit exactly where he said it would be, Vivian took a second to look at herself in the mirror. She didn't look upset, insulted or homeless. She had a smattering of makeup left and her eyes weren't red from crying for once.

Since the rain had stopped, her hair was actually halfway decent, too. She washed her hands, grabbed a clean washcloth and towel, then returned to the living room.

Slate did indeed have his pants pulled down around his boots. His strong thighs were tan instead of the white that she would expect from someone who worked out in the sun instead of going tanning. He also had a pillow covering his lap.

"I'll clean up in here while you're getting your stuff together," he said.

She hadn't noticed that the living room was still a mess from the earlier fight. Had that really been just a few hours ago? She pulled the coffee table closer, opened everything and caught a look at Slate's knees.

"Those are pretty bad. There're rocks still in the wounds." She retrieved a bowl of warm water and a beer for the patient. "This is going to hurt. No way around it."

"Yeah, I figured."

The peroxide fizzed and she instinctively blew and waved her fingers at the white bubbles. She used the cloth to clean as much as she could before using the tweezers for the pebbles stuck in his skin. It was an intense experience and the least she could do for Slate after keeping Allan Pinkston from catching her.

Had Slate known he'd wreck his knees like this in the gravel?

He gritted his teeth, took a sip of beer and dug his nails into the pillow. But he never yelled out. Vivian hated hurting him and winced several times at what she had to do.

"Thank you," she whispered when she finished taping the second bandage in place.

"I think you've got that backward." He reached for the top of his pants but paused.

"If I were you, I'd get something looser than those jeans. At least for tonight."

He splayed his hands like he was stuck. She tugged the jeans up a bit, giving her access to the boots. Then she slipped each from a foot before pulling off the jeans, then folding them. She set them on the arm of the couch and extended her hands to help him stand. Much like he'd done for her before Pinkston had arrived.

He took her hands and when she tugged, his body rose to be next to hers. She couldn't step back because of the table. His arms went around her waist to prevent her from falling.

Close to him again, she felt all the tension leave her body to be replaced by anticipation. She wanted him all over again. His erection proved he wanted her, too.

"I'm sorry if I offended you back in the truck," he said softly. "I was embarrassed for the both of us. Not that we had anything to be embarrassed about. We're both adults. It was just that it wasn't fair to you that my parents...you know."

"We've already agreed that sleeping together isn't the most brilliant idea right now."

"Probably not. But you should understand that it's still on my to-do list. You're not getting away that easily."

"I didn't think I had been affected by everything in the past couple of days, but you may be right. I mean, right about being emotionally compromised." She sweetly kissed his lips and kept it short. "I don't mind being on your to-do list."

She was certain that could be misinterpreted, but she didn't care. They were friends again. She was curious about the potential between them and knew he understood. He stepped around her and gestured toward his boxers.

"I should probably get some running pants on before Dad comes looking for me."

"Couldn't we stay here? I hate to impose on your parents."

"No imposition. We're expected and we both need some sleep." He cupped her chin in his hand. "If we stay here, we both know sleep is the last thing we'll be getting."

He lifted his laptop.

"Is it broken?" she asked.

"Nothing a good charge won't fix. I'll pack it up so we can get the list update from Heath or Wade in the morning."

Slate got dressed, they gathered everything, straightened the room a little and then they settled in at the main house, where fresh brownies were waiting.

Vivian didn't have to wonder how Slate became such an awesome guy. She was blown away by the generosity of all of the Thompson family. She'd never be able to repay their kindness but she was going to try.

Chapter Twenty-One

Abby put the final touches into the white-noise program for the patients who would visit the EEG lab the next day. Her time was limited in the Dallas lab. Her next round of patients would be in Arizona. The movers had been hired to pack up the house.

Of course, her sensitive research would travel directly with her. Not in the moving trucks her father had scheduled for the end of the week.

Sometimes it was great to have her father's money. He was glad to pay for the move to her first job in Texas. Basically, it had been farther away from them in Florida. The Veterans Hospital in Arizona was one of the largest in the country and she wouldn't limit herself to a certain caliber of patient.

As soon as she programmed the last two names on the sleep-study list today, she'd be ready to leave Texas.

It was hard to add an activity to her routine, but she wanted to know if Allan Pinkston had carried out his mission. There wasn't a mention of an attack on a Texas Ranger, but she couldn't rule him out yet. There was still time before he'd been programmed to eliminate himself.

She looked in the mirror, but the woman there was silent.

No voice of reason. Only thoughts of panic.

How had she failed?

She needed her answers. Maybe switching to another facility with additional patients wasn't enough. She trimmed her cuticles, washed her hands, scrubbed under the nails and up her arms with her surgical brush. The stiff bristles indicated cleanliness. She strove toward that perfect sterile world and she'd get there soon.

Chapter Twenty-Two

"Slate Hansom, it's time for lunch. We'd like to eat and be cleared away before we leave for Oklahoma." His mom untied her apron and left it on the back of her chair. "Investigative work sure does look boring."

She'd cooked enough food to last them a week. She and his dad would be gone through Monday, and Slate really hoped he'd have this case wrapped up by then to keep his parents out of danger. Last night had been close.

"It not only looks that way, it definitely is," Vivian agreed.

"We've gotten a lot accomplished this morning. It beats knocking on twenty doors, driving all over the metroplex and hoping people are home. Now we've got three solid interviews lined up."

"Sounds good, son." His dad patted him across the back before sitting at the table. He'd already finished his chores, packed the car and showered.

His father had worked all his life. Hard work on the ranch, holding off selling any of it until it was evident that he and his sister didn't want to raise horses and give lessons.

"Did you get in touch with your half of the list, Viv?" Slate asked.

"We meet with the last one tomorrow at eleven during his lunch break." She smiled and lifted an eyebrow. "You never did tell me why you're called Hansom."

"It's a family name," his mom chimed in. "Been in the family for generations. We think some family relative must have owned an English carriage. We haven't connected the genealogy back to the man who invented it, though."

"Oh, so you're named after a carriage not your looks," Vivian said for his ears only. She laughed and handed him her list.

It was good to hear her laugh, especially after the tragic stories he'd been hearing all morning. Together they'd found a lot of troubled veterans on the list. His call to the Rockwall PD wasn't encouraging either. Allan Pinkston still couldn't remember why he was stalking Vivian or why he'd attacked them twice. There was something about the wild look in his eyes that made Slate think he wasn't completely in control of himself.

After the police conversation, he'd begun calling the men and women on the list to ask if they were having blackouts, periods of time they couldn't remember getting to or from someplace. He sent a text message to the other rangers so they could add the question to their own lists.

Called to lunch a third time, Slate stopped at his

dining table chair, sending another text about his and Vivian's progress.

"Honey, I know you're a grown man, but having your phone out at the table is just rude," his mother reprimanded. "You know how much I dislike it."

He turned his phone facedown and dropped his napkin in his lap. "If Heath or Jack call, I've got to take it, Mom. Just giving you a heads-up."

Lunch was more like a full dinner, including cloth napkins normally reserved for Sunday. Chicken strips, mashed potatoes and gravy, along with corn on the cob and biscuits. He'd smelled the chocolate chip cookies and snitched a couple earlier while they were cooling. He'd even shared with Vivian.

They passed the food and his parents kept looking at Vivian's almost-empty plate. "Aren't you hungry, dear?" his mom asked.

"I'm still full from the wonderful breakfast you made us. I'm not used to eating every meal of the day."

"Well, it's good you're with us then. We'll get some meat on your bones."

There was nothing wrong with the amount of meat on Vivian's bones. She was excellent and he hoped he got another chance to tell her, to show her.

"Come on, Mom. She's not ten. She'll eat if she's hungry." As soon as his plate was loaded, his phone rang. He picked it up along with a chicken tender and walked to the porch.

"Thompson." Unable to resist, he took a large bite of the tender.

"Jack and I are on our way to the ranch," Heath said, like that was the plan.

"Don't eat. Mom cooked." Heath would know there was enough here to feed an army. Slate's mother never cooked in half measures.

"Works for me. You're not going to believe what we've stumbled into."

"I think I will. What's your ETA?"

"Less than twenty."

Back at the table with his phone facedown again, he shoveled the food into his mouth. "Eat up, Vivian. The guys will be here to combine all the data. We'll clear and clean, Mom. You guys need to hit the road before traffic."

And before his coworkers arrived. His parents finished and hugged him goodbye. Then they hugged Vivian. No surprise. She was officially part of the household...almost family by his mother's definition.

"Good luck with your brother's case. We'll be thinking about you and praying that you both stay safe." His dad was normally the succinct man of few words. Sometime that morning, he'd gotten Vivian to talk about what they were doing.

"Take care of yourself, Slate. We told your sister to stay at school this weekend and we've canceled the riding lessons. Remember that you're in charge of the livestock."

"Yes, ma'am. Heath and I will take care of it."

"I'll help. You guys have a safe trip." Vivian waved from the porch.

And then they were gone. He was once again alone

with Vivian. Not for long, but alone. He'd botched his apology last night and then she'd cleaned his knees. She'd insisted on taking a look at them this morning and debriding them again. His mom got a look and told him to go to the doctor.

The morning's events flashed through his mind in the couple of seconds it took to walk back up the three steps to the porch where she stood holding the screen door open. But a vision of the future beckoned to him of her doing the same thing.

Why? He barely knew this woman. But he wanted to know her better, wanted her to stay and be comfortable. Not only at his place, but also his parents' house. That meant something, right?

He wasn't a monk. Far from it. He'd had his fair share of dates and girlfriends. But never anything this intense, this fast. Proven last night when he'd forgotten about their situation and let his guard down.

Dammit. He liked Vivian Watts. A lot.

"Time to clean up?" Vivian asked.

"Huh?" He literally had to shake himself to stop dwelling on how fast this was hitting him. "Um, not yet. I told the guys there was food."

"I hope they have a plan. Victor is running out of time."

They went back to the den where they'd been making their calls. There was still a landline in this room for emergencies, which Vivian used. She checked the list and had the receiver up to dial.

"Wait," he said. "You know we're getting closer.

Think where you were three days ago. You were just waiting for the trial to happen with no hope."

"All I can see is how far we still have to go."

"You have help now. People who care about making certain justice is carried out and that an innocent man doesn't stay behind bars."

He meant it. They both made another call. The families on the other end of the line were anxious to talk with someone about the injustices their loved ones had experienced. It was disheartening to listen to the same story—different variations, but basically the same story—about forgotten heroes.

The porch screen door squeaked open and closed.

"Do I smell chicken?" Heath didn't wait for an invitation to enter.

Jack followed Heath to the table. Both of his friends filled their plates and said no when Vivian offered to warm up the food.

"Something is definitely wrong with this sleep study. Almost half of the men and women on our list have had an altercation with the police in the past six months," Heath said, dipping his chicken into the gravy. "Man, your mom can cook. Let me see your list."

"It's about the same," Vivian said. "Almost half. We each spoke with a wife who had lost her husband in a murder-suicide. One killed a stranger and one killed a stranger off the street."

"I had one," Jack said. "He killed a grocery clerk for giving him the incorrect change, according to witnesses."

"What are the odds of that happening to three men in the same sleep study?" Vivian asked.

"Pretty damn low," Jack threw out.

"Are we one hundred percent certain that we have all the correct patients?" Slate put the question out there, but Heath nodded as he ate, acknowledging he'd done the work correctly. "Man, name after name kept coming up with a problem. One's involved with a brawl and the next is associated with a domestic dispute. By the time I got to the fifth name on my list, it was clear something was wrong."

"Good grief." Heath held up all three lists. "Did you realize that the only man affected out of alphabetical order is your brother?"

"Do the dates they had a brush with the law match alphabetically?"

Heath arched his eyebrows as he read and began nodding. "Pretty much."

"How can someone be getting these honorable men and women to break the law? Do you think it's without their knowledge?"

"Hypnotism?"

"Or something worse. It's a damn sleep study. What if someone's experimenting on them?" Heath was serious.

"That's ridiculous. It couldn't possibly happen without someone knowing about it," Vivian said. "Right?"

"I just looked it up and found a dozen sites on sleep programming to rewire your brain. I guess it's not so ridiculous." Heath kept typing on his laptop.

"Do you think Dr. Roberts was brainwashing veterans during a sleep study?" Vivian asked.

Heath shook his head. "The timing is off. Her murder was eleven months ago. The police reports don't go back that far."

"So we're still looking for Subject Nineteen," Slate pointed out.

"If you take Victor out of the equation, what's the connection? Who wants her dead?" Jack asked before munching down on another cookie.

"All of Dr. Roberts's associates were accounted for—they had alibis. She didn't have a boyfriend. She didn't have a husband or ex-husband or even an ex-boyfriend. We need to find Subject Nineteen. Male or female, this person is the key and probably the murderer." Slate paced around the room, very aware that everyone was listening.

"We have to go to the old man." Jack leaned back from the table. "This isn't just about seeing if Victor Watts is innocent. We need an official investigation."

"How long will that take?" she asked. Heath and Jack looked away. "My brother's trial begins Monday."

Slate barely had the courage to look her in the eye. "What choice do we have? We need an official investigation to get through the door, to ask doctors, nurses, janitors if they think something weird is going on."

"That might take weeks. If he enters a plea of guilty, he loses his right to appeal. No. There has to be another way."

"First, we get assigned the case. We talk with the VA OIG." Jack was the practical ranger. The one who knew the rules and how everything worked.

"Who?"

"The VA's Office of Inspector General. They'd handle complaints and investigations to see what's going on," Heath explained. "They don't like to share or play well with others."

"And if they say no? What then?" Vivian asked.

Slate crossed the small distance to stand next to her and face his friends. "She's right. Whatever happens with the bureaucracy, it'll be too late to help Victor. He's innocent."

"You *hope* he's innocent." Jack shrugged. "We all hope he's innocent but our hands are tied on this now. Whatever strange thing is happening in connection with the sleep study these veterans are a part of, we have to build a case by proceeding with authority. We need permission to get at those doctors and the rest of the staff."

"The VA inspector isn't going to cooperate." Heath shook his head before standing and ticking things off on his fingers. "The first thing they'll do is shut down the study. Then they'll drag their feet because they lack the staff or need to bring in a specialist from DC to ask the questions. In turn, that will alert whoever's messing with these veterans. They'll disappear before the investigation even gets started."

"That's not necessarily the case."

Slate shot Jack a get-real look. They all knew about government bureaucracy.

"What I meant…" Jack shrugged and continued "…is that we could get someone into the study undercover before we tell anyone."

"It's too late for that," Heath countered. "First, the person manipulating these people probably knows all about us. And second, the study's nearly over. They won't let anyone else enter it at this point."

"But my brother is out of time. Face it, this explanation doesn't sound believable enough for the sci-fi channel to make a movie about it. Who do we approach and how do we get them to believe us?"

"I think we should go to the old man with a plan. It's too important to just wing it." Slate knew it was the only way. He'd call and set up an appointment. He would take all the heat.

No one would get in trouble for working on this case without authority...except Slate.

"We get Major Clements to convince them to send one of us in undercover. Has to be tomorrow. We find out what tests are required from the sleep-study patients, get us moved to the head of the line and get a handle on all the personnel."

"It should be me." Heath dipped his chin but raised a finger. "I'm the least likely to be recognized. They obviously know who you are, Slate. Jack, your father just won the senate race and you were in the news again last week. So it has to be me."

"Fine," Slate said at the same time Jack agreed.

"I've got all the data together and will print out the summary for Major Clements." Heath slapped Slate on his back on his way out the door. "By the way, you're not taking all the heat on this. I'll be at the meeting."

"So will I." Jack gripped Slate's hand. "We're in this together."

"You know, statistically, every ten days a murder is committed that won't ever be solved."

"Coming from Heath, that's probably true," Jack said before getting into his truck.

Vivian stood next to Slate, waiting for his friends to leave. Slate wanted to put his arm around her, to offer comfort. But that was too dangerous now that they were alone.

"Killing by a stranger. Do you really think someone is programming men to kill people they don't know? It's like *Strangers on a Train*. There'd be no way to connect the murderer to the murder."

"If it worked, if the veteran never remembered anything or if they commit suicide, then we might be looking at the perfect murder."

Chapter Twenty-Three

Vivian had reluctantly been allowed in the back of the major's office after she'd promised not to interject information or beg for her brother. It was hard, but she'd managed. Jack and Heath had also managed not to say anything, even with all the harrumphs the older ranger had made throughout Slate's convincing argument.

"Domestic violence, drunk and disorderly conduct, trespassing, voyeurism, and then there are the three murder-suicides in the past six weeks," Slate stated their case.

Or maybe it was a plea. If she'd been allowed to speak, Vivian would be crying and begging, attempting to convince the older Texas Ranger that her brother had to be innocent. There was a possibility that had occurred to her on the ride over to Company B. She didn't voice it out loud and didn't want to think about it. But her brother might have committed the murder after being brainwashed or reprogrammed.

However the Rangers wanted to refer to it didn't matter. She couldn't bear to think Victor was actually guilty. Judging him wasn't her job. Pleading for his innocence and being his sister was.

"That's why we need to get in there and find out what's going on, sir." Slate finished a very well-presented summary of their last week.

"Wade's behind this. He asked you to look into another one of his hunches," Major Clements muttered, but he didn't demand an answer.

Would the man in charge call it quits if Slate admitted that Wade was behind reopening the case?

"As I said, sir, I began looking into this on my own time. I met Vivian when I had lunch at the restaurant where she worked. After we were attacked a second time, I asked Jack and Heath for help to look at the situation more closely. That's when we discovered how many veterans had been affected."

Facts. He stated facts without involving Wade.

"You brought it to me." The commander leaned back in his chair, contemplating. "You know my hands are tied on this. I have to turn your findings over to the inspector general of the VA."

"We assumed that but were hoping—"

"What? That I'd convince the OIG to let you interview their doctors and patients? That's not the way things are done in government, especially at the VA."

Slate nodded but stood straight. No hand gestures, no fidgeting. And no looking around the room at her or his friends.

Vivian stood perfectly still, too. Trying not to draw attention to herself was getting harder and harder. Her lip was raw from biting down on it. What would she do if the major decided against fighting for her brother? Shout? Scream out? Cry?

Do it herself? Alone?

She would if she only knew where to begin. In fact, she would have already. Slate's comment at lunch about how far they'd come in the past couple of days was right. She'd been floundering on her own for months. Two days working with him and his friends, and they might actually get her brother freed.

It all depended on the man behind the desk. The man these rangers—standing around her, who had helped her—respected and trusted.

Major Clements rubbed his chin with his thumb and finger. "I respect you, Thompson. I'm going to make a couple of calls. No promises. And don't think this debate about how you came across this case is finished."

"Thank you, sir."

Jack and Heath turned, pulled the office door open and both put a hand on her back for her to go in front of them. She walked through with no idea where to go until she caught Wade's small hand wave in what appeared to be a break room.

"How did it go?" Wade asked under his breath, bringing his head close to hers.

"The major's at least making the call to the VA. That's hopeful." She kept her voice down, too.

"Sorry."

At first, Vivian didn't completely understand why Wade would be sorry. Then she caught a glance of Slate's expression. His eyes were drawn together, his brow wrinkled and strained, his lips pressed flat together...

Jealousy?

Wade winked at her and moved to the soda machine. Slate kept staring at him. And yes, it seemed like he was giving him the back-off evil eye. She'd seen the possessive look once or twice in her life. Just not recently.

It was a nice feeling and caused her to smile. She needed to be reminded that life went on, even if hers had practically stopped for the past year. She and Victor would come out of this ready to move forward. She'd be there for him this time.

She wouldn't let anything come between a new relationship with her brother. Sadly, that included Slate. He had a younger sister. He'd understand why Victor would come first in her life.

Wade, Heath and Jack all had assignments they needed to work. Slate was officially on paid leave. Vivian fiddled with her visitor badge while Slate looked at his phone.

"Mom and Dad checked in to their hotel."

"Glad they made it okay."

Vivian wanted to talk about the plan to help the VA's office find out what was happening within the study. Or talk about the look Slate had given Wade. Instead, she got into her head, thinking what would happen if she didn't free Victor.

"Do you think you should interview Victor?" she asked. "He might have some important information."

"Heath went to interview him yesterday. As the arresting officer, he set it up with that scumbag lawyer."

Slate was right about Ned Stevens, and after her brother was released, she'd file a complaint with someone…somewhere. After. Everything was about *after*.

"Thank you. No matter what happens. Thank you for everything you've done."

"Except the almost-getting-you-killed parts." He swiped a hand across his face, covering his eyes from her.

"No." She touched his hand, looking at him so he knew she meant it. "Those incidents made me remember where I'm from and where I've been."

"Which is where? You've met my parents and seen not only baby pictures but also goofy teen pictures when I was sweating in marching band. You practically know my life story."

"You know about the whole foster situation and I can't tell you it was all grand. Being separated from my brother was a relief at first. I mean, I was only sixteen and he was eleven—completely my responsibility. I wanted to hate them for separating us, but couldn't. But then I was crazy guilty. The only reason I joined the military was for the training and college opportunities. I couldn't take care of Victor without a way to provide for us both."

Their hands were still connected. He turned his palm up and laced his fingers through hers. It was comforting while they waited and got to know each other a little.

"I get the guilt. My story's different, but I'm not taking over my parents' dream. That's a lot of to be responsible for. Back to your story."

"Right. I stood in your living room more embarrassed than helpless. I served four years in the army. Basic was hard, but it toughened me up. I can fight, Slate. I won't be huddled in the corner next time."

He smiled and nodded as if he were wondering whether to believe her or not. This wasn't the time or place, but she'd like to get him on a workout mat. She could show him a move or two.

It was close to five o'clock when Major Clements gathered them back in his office. Once again, she stood near the door in the background, hoping no one would object to her involvement.

"It's a go. We've just got one hitch." The major looked at each of the men. "You need to find someone who's a veteran. We don't have time to go through all the channels to set up a fake history."

"What about James Diaz? Didn't he serve in the military?"

"I think Taylor White was in the National Guard."

"I can do it," Vivian volunteered quietly. She wasn't supposed to speak out. Doing so drew everyone's attention to her. "I served in the army."

"No way. The person behind this will know you on sight. What if you get programmed to shoot yourself?" Slate's attitude was full of emotion. He'd controlled himself throughout the day and especially the afternoon. His reaction was unexpected.

"You'll be with me to keep anything bad from happening. I'm the logical person, I know what to look for. And if it makes the person harming everyone run, then you'll all be there to catch them."

"No one has more at risk than her. And she's right. She does have us to look out for her." Jack spoke to the major, pointedly ignoring Slate's outburst.

"Doesn't it defeat the purpose of being undercover if the person we're after knows her?" Slate tried again.

"We're out of time, man." Heath looked at his partner and then at his commanding officer. "Sir, she does have military background. It's not the same as sending in an untrained civilian."

Major Clements had crossed his arms over his chest and looked at her while the men argued. It was his decision and his eyes locked with hers.

"Will it work?" she asked him.

"There are risks. You aren't law enforcement. Where did you serve?"

"Afghanistan for eight months and no, it wasn't in the typing pool." Everyone except Slate laughed. "I know my way around a weapon, but I won't need one in the hospital. I can do whatever's necessary. It's for my brother."

"Get it set up."

"But, sir, this—"

"You may not like it, Thompson, but you need to make it happen and be thorough."

"I'd like permission to accompany Miss Watts. I can go in as her fiancé or husband. If the person behind this knows who she is, it won't matter if he sees me with her."

"You're right. As soon as he recognizes Miss Watts, he'll know why you're there. But being known as her husband would keep you close to observe not only her reactions, but the reactions of the staff." The major clapped his hand on Slate's shoulder.

"It's quicker to get you the necessary documents fixed up so you look like newlyweds than military records." Heath picked up his phone and made a call. "I suggest we give you a head injury, Vivian, and say you're having trouble sleeping."

"You don't have to do this," Slate tried again. "Give us an hour and we can find a ranger who is also a veteran."

"It's okay, Slate. I told you, I can handle it."

"Will you keep looking for someone more qualified?" he asked Jack, who just shook his head. "She hasn't exactly shown all this skill she claims to have."

"This is the best way, Slate. Posing as her husband, you can be there with her for every diagnosis and plan of action. There's no way we could set up that kind of scenario if it was Taylor White." Heath was still on the phone but slapped Slate on the back. "You know this, man."

"I might know it, but I don't have to like it."

Vivian stood next to Slate's desk. She'd intended to fill Wade in, but Slate's reaction had her confused. But she wouldn't let wondering about his intentions mess up how excited she was to finally participate in helping her brother.

"So…you want to marry me?" she whispered, gently sending an elbow into Slate's ribs.

"You might say that. But first we're hitting the gym."

Was he worried that she'd mess things up or worried that something might happen to her? Another crazy impression, but she got the feeling it was the latter.

Chapter Twenty-Four

"This isn't exactly how I envisioned our first date." Slate looked up from the floor mat into a pair of steel-gray eyes. "Can you change the color by changing your mood?"

"No. My eyes do whatever they want." Vivian laughed and extended a hand to help him to his feet. "How much longer do I have to show you that I'm capable of defending myself?"

"I believed you the first time my back hit this mat." He popped to his feet a little slower but ready to go again. "Nothing wrong with a little practice."

"Okay, but there's also a thing about rubbery arms if something happens for real."

Each strike he threw, she blocked correctly. The kick he sent her way, she dodged predictably. It was later in the day. No one was in the gym except them. No one would interrupt.

Slate needed to catch her off guard. See what she would do in an impossible situation. He pulled her to him, dropping his guard with his arms circling her waist. He latched his thumbs through her belt loops, trapping her arms at her sides. She tried to break free. This time, he didn't want her to get away.

"No fair."

"Get free." He tried to keep the smile off his face and laughter from his voice.

"Slate, attackers aren't going to hug me."

"Get free or say uncle."

"Um… I don't say uncle." She twisted.

He kept her next to his chest.

She raised a knee. He blocked with his hip but still kept his grip. She pulled, twisted, jerked and moved in ways that were a complete turn-on…but she still didn't get free.

Vivian brushed the back of her hand across his groin. He was expecting a reluctant word of surrender or apology when she tilted her face toward his and kissed him.

Thoroughly.

And again. Their mouths slashed, transferring the sparring energy from their bodies to their lips. Nothing but explosive energy between them existed. If his thumbs hadn't been hooked in her belt loops, he might have stood a chance. But this way? He couldn't untangle himself before she was paying him back for his torture of her the night before.

Exquisite torture he not only wanted, but craved.

Time and place didn't matter much when it came to male body parts. Tight blue jeans might have helped him from immediately expanding, but the loose work-out sweats gave him room to grow.

Damn it.

Stopping her was what he should do. Okay, so he

didn't really want to stop her, but this wasn't what he had in mind. Vivian's fingers skimmed over his collarbone. Then her fingernail scraped the outline of his earlobe.

When had her arms become free?

Vivian leaned into him, bringing her full body in contact with his. She turned her hip past the drawstring dangling from his pants. Full-blown erection. He had to keep her close in case someone walked in.

It didn't help his erection any that he'd wanted Vivian since the moment he'd seen her in the chicken wing uniform.

Remembering how she'd reacted to his touches didn't help his body respond any less either. He wanted to throw her to the mat and encourage those reactions again.

Their eyes met and he saw her smile—a smile of determination. No matter what she might say, she'd done that on purpose. But there were cameras.

"Uncle," he whispered. "The owners can see us."

They broke apart—too soon in his humble opinion—both still breathing rapidly.

He kept his mouth close to hers as he said, "I have to admit that was an unusual solution to your problem. No one I know would have approached it that way."

"And not a move that would work on everyone. Honestly, I don't know how that happened. I was thinking a head butt and the next thing I knew, I was leaning another direction." She ran her fingernails up and down his back.

He freed his thumbs and circled her slender waist with his fingers. She was free, but didn't move away.

"The head butt would have worked and was sort of what I was prepared for." He brushed her lips one last time, putting space between their bodies. "This was much more pleasant."

"I guess we should get cleaned up and head to the hospital. We don't have time for anything else. Right?"

"Time? Yes. Should we? No."

"Oh." She backed away with a disappointed look and he had to catch her hand, circling her back to him.

"Will it happen? Yes, absolutely, don't doubt it." He kissed her long and sumptuously, putting more of himself into the effort than he had for anyone. "That's a promise, ma'am. And I don't break my promises."

"Good to know, ranger."

SLATE DIDN'T THINK this operation would go south. He knew it would. They weren't prepared. They weren't in control. And he was crazy about the woman sitting next to him. As in, so major crazy it would cause problems if she were in danger.

He couldn't think straight and they hadn't done anything except fill out some papers for the hospital.

Jack and Heath waited in their vehicle a couple of blocks away. Wade was still at Company B headquarters. Their plan of action was to go through the emergency room and get most of the preliminary exams out of the way throughout the night.

Vivian had to be admitted the good old-fashioned way before their OIG contact could put her to the head of the line for the head-injury-specific tests. Tests that should be similar to those needed in the sleep study. Their contact would also make certain that the doctors performing those tests or exams were the same.

"I feel guilty taking time away from these men and women who need the care like my brother." Vivian was doing a great job acting nervous…or maybe she just wasn't pretending to be calm.

"What about the men and women who are a part of the study and not able to function in normal life? Just think about the three men who committed suicide and the many other innocent victims."

"Done. We're here for a purpose." She looked around the room. "Greater than my brother now."

"Damn straight."

They waited several hours before the basic tests began. After being up all night, it wasn't hard to look tired or be discouraged that they weren't going home. Nine o'clock rolled around and they'd been in the hospital ten hours, seeing doctors for four of them.

No one could find anything wrong with Vivian. Of course, there wasn't anything wrong.

"How ya doing?" Wade asked during a phone call for an update.

"They're still digging around for answers," Slate said from the waiting room.

"Well, the people working on Vivian's case should be getting a couple of urgent care requests fairly soon."

They disconnected. Vivian was resting her head on his shoulder, so he kept the phone in his hand. Someone with a clipboard walked by, pointed to his phone and shook their head. This was one rule he'd be breaking. They'd given Jack's phone to Vivian in case they got separated.

God, he hoped this plan worked. Would they really be able to spook whoever was brainwashing patients? Hopefully spook them into running instead of doing something to Vivian.

"Watts. Vivian Watts," a nurse called her name, waking her.

She pushed up from his shoulder and they both walked to the door.

"Sorry. No one but the patient can go back."

"You can't make an exception?" he asked.

"No." The nurse held out a hand, stopping him. "She'll be fine. We'll take good care of her."

Slate pulled her to him for a hug and whispered, "Text me where you are. I'll find a way back there."

She nodded and he kissed her cheek. The door closed and once again he found himself praying that his gut instinct about this operation was wrong.

Chapter Twenty-Five

Abby got her list of patients for the day, dropped the clipboard and had to apologize. She quickly picked it up, holding it in her gloved hand, and just as quickly ran to the ladies' room.

"What is she doing on my list of patients?" She asked the question several times expecting the answer. Nothing came.

Was the woman in the mirror disappointed in the mistakes that had been made? Is that why she wasn't imparting the right path? Allan Pinkston was a disappointment, she thought, then said it out loud, attempting to begin the conversation.

"We do not have resources to waste at this time to eliminate her," the perfect voice finally answered.

"You know if she's here for a test, then he's not far away."

"If you run the experiment on her, then they'll find you. Our research will be over. We won't ever be together."

"But she must be eliminated."

"There are other ways. You have cash. Use it. You

have access to drugs…procure them. Use your head, girl. Stop being a ninny."

That wasn't perfection. Those words were cruelty itself. Her father. The voice in the mirror was gone. She was on her own to find someone to deal with this matter.

She had until one o'clock before Victor's sister was getting nodes attached to her head. Abby hated to be off schedule. It would send her day into disarray. She wanted neatly run, smooth, orderly clockwork. Everything had a place. The things she did had a time to do them.

She could deviate from the daily schedule today in order to get the annoyance out of the picture. She used the stairs to arrive in the emergency department. She pulled her mask over her mouth and nose and ventured into the emergency room to recruit help.

Chapter Twenty-Six

Wrapped in a paper gown and blanket, Vivian sat in a hall for at least half an hour before anyone said, "Follow me." She went into a waiting room with lockers and was instructed to put her clothes and everything with her—including Jack's cell—into the locker of her choice. Each locker had a key that could be worn around your wrist.

"This is going to drive Slate so crazy," she mumbled to herself.

The idea of keeping in touch with him evaporated into the bad-smelling spray someone had used in the corner.

She was on her own—completely on her own—through the first test. But she'd had an MRI before. Nothing went wrong. Her brain was still there, according to the doctors. In an aside, the technician said everything looked good, but the doctor would give her the results later.

Vivian didn't find anything or anyone in the area suspicious. It didn't look like anyone would have an opportunity to brainwash a veteran. She wondered about that. Heath had mentioned sleep tapes. So whoever was possibly hurting the patients would need to have an extended period of private time with them.

It seemed like a logical conclusion. At least to herself. She'd have to go with it since there was no one else to ask. She was waiting to be escorted to her next test. The people around her seemed to treat her with kid gloves. She had to wonder what story the OIG had told to everyone.

She flipped through the only magazine on the table, reading just about every article and advertisement inside. She was starving and super tired, but she continued to wait. She slapped the magazine down on the table.

A lot of people had gone to a lot of trouble for today to happen. It didn't matter if she was hungry and wanted a certain bed in a certain ranger's home.

"Miss Watts?" a woman with a clipboard asked.

"That's me." She felt silly for answering since no one was in the waiting area with her.

"I was hoping you were here. Word came down to work you in for an EEG today. We're running ahead of schedule and thought we squeeze you in. Come this way."

Vivian followed the woman down the hall and into the elevator.

"What's an EEG?"

"It's used to monitor brain activity. Basically, we put gel on your scalp, connect a bunch of electrodes to your head and monitor you for a while. It's harmless and completely noninvasive. The worst part about my test is that you need to wash your hair afterward."

They got off the elevator on the fifth floor. Her guide opened a door and gestured for Vivian to go inside. "Abby will get you all prepped. I'll be back in a few minutes to get the test started."

"Oh, hi." Vivian recognized the woman who had spoken to her and Slate just two days earlier. "I think we met a couple of days ago."

"Oh, my gosh, you're the woman from the cafeteria. You were with that tall Texas Ranger. You know I'd never met one of them before. He's quite handsome."

"Slate is great."

"Were you both working on Rashid's case for some reason?"

"Actually, Slate is a friend. I mean husband. It's all so new. We just got married." Hopefully that explanation covered her mistake. "He brought me to the hospital because I fell and hit my head. While he was here, he got curious and started asking questions about the attack."

It was the story they'd agreed on. If anyone asked, they'd come here for her, not because of any case.

"I have to say that they got you in for testing fast. Your name must be on someone's favorite list. Things usually move real slow around here." Abby picked up a clipboard. "I have to ask you some boring questions that you've probably already answered. Everything's routine and I have to write it down again for our charts. Okay?"

"So that's the part you do?"

"Questions, and I get to attach the connector node goo. I've enjoyed working here and decided to go back to school to become a certified lab technician to perform the test myself. I find it very interesting. Now, you said you hit your head?"

"Yes, and I've had trouble sleeping since then."

"Any loss of consciousness or sign of a seizure?"

"No, I'm learning to ride horses and fell."

"Oh, my. I hope you got right back on it."

Vivian nodded and answered all the same questions about her head injury. The one difference in this department was that Abby used a clipboard with real paper. All the other departments had input the information directly onto a portable tablet.

She wanted to ask about it but was busy observing the assistant. There was an artificial awkwardness emanating from her movements and words. She smiled, but it was carefully in all the right pauses. She giggled, but it didn't quite seem real.

So was the assistant's behavior strained because she was covering something up? Or strained because she knew Slate was a Texas Ranger? It could be simply because Vivian as a patient had been labeled a VIP. Or none of it could mean anything and it could all be wishful thinking on Vivian's part.

How could a person investigating something on this scale tell which idea to follow? Make her own judgment call? Wait for feedback from the rest of the team? Perhaps she lacked the experience to discover anything useful after meeting all of these potential suspects. How would she narrow her impressions down to a manageable number?

Abby continued to part Vivian's hair and apply the spots of gel that would hold the electric nodes in place for the test. She was either concentrating very hard on a procedure that she'd done hundreds of times or ignoring normal conversation.

Why did the assistant's movements and expressions feel calculated? Was it just Vivian's desire that somebody she met today be worthy of an investigation? Or was it Vivian projecting her need to have someone seem guilty?

First thing, she had to calm down and go through all the motions. There wasn't a mirror, just a one-way glass at the end of the room. She looked very strange with her hair parted in rows, white gel that looked like toothpaste in dots across her head.

"So what happens now?"

"Lucy will be back any minute. She'll add the actual electric nodes and then she'll begin the test."

"What do I do?"

"Well, a lot of people fall asleep. We get the best results when you're relaxed."

"I've been up all night. A nap sounds extremely good right now."

"Would you like a bottle of water?" Abby reached into a small fridge and handed her a small bottle of mineral water.

"That would be great. Thanks."

Lucy came into the room and finished the preparations. She began the test, checked the EEG machine and told Abby she'd return in about half an hour.

Abby dimmed the lights and pulled the door almost closed. Vivian was thirsty and emptied the bottle of water. Then she closed her eyes and that was it. She awoke totally refreshed when Lucy touched her shoulder.

"My goodness, you were so sound asleep," the technician said. "Let's get you cleaned up now."

"I don't remember falling asleep."

"Well, apparently you needed a bit of rest. Good for you." She pulled wires, wiped the gel and then gave Vivian a disposable comb to pull through her tangles.

Abby waved from her desk when she left with Lucy to go back to the waiting area on the third floor. She walked into the room to find an almost frantic Slate.

He pulled her into his arms and hugged her, kissing her forehead. "Dammit, I've been worried."

"You look like you should have had that last test. I fell asleep and feel great now. Completely refreshed and ready for the next thing." She pulled away and looked at him. "I thought you were supposed to wait downstairs?"

"Yeah, well after the first hour that just wasn't going to work for me. I finally slipped through the doors. It took me a couple of hours to find this room."

"You must have just missed me before I left for the EEG." She ran her hands through her hair. "I feel like I have conditioner in my hair now. It's so greasy."

"Are you okay?" They sat in two chairs in the corner.

"Yes. I know my hair's a mess, but I feel great. Don't I look okay?"

"As a matter of fact, you do. It's just that…"

"I haven't found anything. Everyone's been nice and accommodating. They're treating me like a VIP…" she lowered her voice "…because they think I am."

"No one gave you any drugs or shots?"

"Nope." Vivian slapped her thighs, twisting in her seat, wanting to press her body next to this gorgeous man. *What am I doing?* "Slate, could we just get out of here?"

"Are you sure no one gave you anything?"

"Positive." She slipped her hand from her leg onto his thigh. "Maybe we could just find an empty room."

She did feel good. *Too good.*

"That's it. Something's wrong." He jumped up, leaving her alone in the corner.

Her skin felt all tingly. Not itching…just tingling and alive. What was wrong with him? She'd seen him in his plaid boxers. Why wouldn't he want to fool around?

Oh, God. Something was completely wrong with her.

Slate opened the door and shouted for a nurse. He pulled his cell from his back pocket and turned to face her again. "Where are your things?"

She lifted her wrist, unable to tell him her locker number in the dressing room behind one of the doors. Not the one he was standing at, but another door. There were lots of words on the tip of her tongue, but none would actually form to create a sentence.

Wow. My mind is totally not in control of anything.

It did wow her that she seemed like two people. One who just observed and one who was stuck, unable to really communicate. She couldn't even point. It was like being stuck in a nightmare, unable to wake up.

Slate rolled the keyring over her wrist. She tried to grab his hand, but he was too fast.

"I'm telling you, someone drugged her. We've got to get her out of here. What do you mean, take her to the emergency room? Whoever did this might be treating her. She's leaving. Meet us at the door."

She shook her head. Back and forth and back and forth until she was dizzy.

Oh, wait. She was more than dizzy…she was about to be sick. Extremely sick. She rose from the chair but fell to her knees.

"Vivian. Can you understand me? Can you even hear me?"

"Bath…" She tried to crawl toward the changing room. "Sick."

After clawing at the carpet a couple of times, attempting to drag herself to the dressing room, she gave up. She just wanted to pass out. Lying on the floor was a very good solution.

Slate picked her up around her waist and practically flew through the door. Her feet barely skimmed the floor he got her there so fast. And just in the nick of time. She lost what little there was in her stomach.

He stayed next to her and handed her paper towels, dabbing at her face and forehead until her own limbs began to obey her orders again. Her mind began clearing as embarrassment set in. Slate whispered into the phone again, probably telling the guys why they weren't downstairs.

He left her alone for a few minutes, and she overheard him talking to a nurse through the door. *My wife this* and *my wife that* didn't completely register as referring to her until Slate returned with towels to clean her up.

Which he did. Alone. He also had a clean hospital gown that he helped her slip into.

"I prefer my own clothes," she managed to tell him.

He ignored her since he didn't dress her. She could barely lift her head from resting on the tiled wall and couldn't argue.

"It's been years and years since I've thrown up. I feel like I've been drinking all night and have a hangover." Vivian dropped her head into her hands, totally at a loss as to why it felt so dang heavy.

"Feeling better?" Slate asked, towering over her.

She couldn't raise her head to convince him she was.

"We're leaving as soon as you can walk to the elevator."

"Clothes?" she asked hopefully.

"The nurse got your bag." He pointed to the one hanging on the back of the door.

"I can get dressed."

"Nope. Not waiting that long."

Completely humiliated by throwing up in front of someone she wanted to find her sexy, she let him wrap his arm around her and leave the waiting area. She was totally out of it. She couldn't even tell if the ties on the gown were done correctly or if the hospital gear was exposing her to the world.

Chapter Twenty-Seven

They were leaving. Walking out. Calling a halt to the operation. The team would punt. Slate was not going to risk Vivian's life again. Who were these monsters? He was about to call Wade and tell him to contact the OIG when the elevator jolted to a halt.

"What's happening? Why are we stopped?"

"Fire!" The shouts were clear even through two sets of steel doors.

Stuck in an elevator while the building was on fire. He checked his cell for reception. Nothing. *Right. Inside an elevator.*

"Do you think someone just pulled the alarm so they could leave the building without us seeing?" she asked.

"We can hope." He popped the emergency call panel open, pushing the button. "No one's answering. We might be on our own."

"Do we need to climb? Is there an escape hatch on the ceiling?"

"Only in the movies. Firefighters have keys, but when an elevator stops, the safest place is inside until they get it moving again." He kept trying the emergency button. The alarm was deafening in their ears, making it difficult to talk.

"Unless there's an actual fire."

"Yeah. But we don't know if it's real. Like you said, someone could have just pulled the alarm." Slate tested the door's open and close buttons again, just to be certain they weren't jammed.

"Either way, people are going to be hurt," Vivian said, sliding down to huddle in the corner. "What if someone is trampled or…or worse? Oh, my God, this is all my fault."

"You didn't pull the fire alarm or set a fire." He sat next to her. Hopefully the smoke would rise inside an elevator, too.

"Actually, you don't know that. I could have set the fire and not remember anything about it. Just like Victor…"

"Feeling any better?"

"Much. I can walk and most important, think." She hugged her hospital-issued plastic sack with her clothes inside.

The alarms were sounding in perfect time on the floors above and below them. They could hear people shouting and running. Everything was amplified inside the elevator shaft.

"Hey, anybody in there?" someone banged on the doors from the hallway. It was faint, but distinct.

They both shouted. Slate kicked their set of doors with his boots.

"Hey! Hey, man! Someone's still in there. Get something to help me!" the voice yelled.

Slate and Vivian waited on the floor, holding hands

after a few minutes. As the doors inched opened, smoke poured inside, replacing the breathable air. They covered their mouths and noses as best they could, but Vivian was still in a hospital gown.

"No matter what happens, you do not leave my side," Slate ordered. "Got it?"

"But—"

"No buts. Just promise."

"Then you go out that door first," she said, matter-of-fact. "You go, you fight if necessary, then you pull me out."

Logical and right. He nodded. If someone had done this deliberately to get at them, then it made sense they would be waiting for them to escape or be rescued.

The fire seemed real. At least, the black smoke swirling above their heads did.

It circled inside the elevator.

The doors were pried and propped open, first in the hallway, then on the elevator itself. The whole process seemed to take hours, but it was just a matter of minutes.

"I'll reach in and get you," Slate promised. "I'll give you a thumbs-up."

She affirmed with a nod. He planted himself between her and the opening, hoping to shield her in case someone just opened fire with a weapon. That was where his mind had gone. Everyone in the hospital was a potential suspect.

But the men who'd pried the doors open were orderlies evacuating everyone off the floor. Good men who pulled him through the opening and helped him do the same for Vivian.

"You okay? Can you walk down the stairs on your own?" one of them asked.

"Thanks and yes," Slate answered, wrapping his arm around Vivian.

The smoke gathered like a fog at the high ceiling but it was still hard to breathe as they got closer to the exit. The sting blurred his vision and his eyes watered. Patients shoved, trying to get through the stairwell door, while hospital employees in scrubs helped those who had fallen or were in wheelchairs.

Slate held his ground, not budging, letting the crush sweep past them. They'd be safer if no one was around. He could protect Vivian better.

"Stay with me," he told her.

Vivian didn't answer so he turned back to check if she was okay.

He didn't see it coming, but he sure as hell felt it hit his shoulder. And it wasn't a stranger. The only person close to him was Vivian. Slate fell to his knees and lifted his arm just in time to deflect another blow from an IV pole that had been left by a patient.

Her eyes were blank, sort of crazy like Allan Pinkston.

"Vivian!"

She threw a jab. He countered with a block. He tried to grab her arms, she evaded. It was like their practice the night before. Almost precisely. What if he repeated his last move?

He took one of her punches to his solar plexus. She wasn't holding anything back, that was for sure. He caught her left arm to her side and struggled to loop his around her right but managed it.

"Vivian!" he shouted, leaning back to avoid the head butt. "Get free, Vivian!"

After a few more seconds of struggling, of lifting her knee and missing, Vivian relaxed like she had the previous evening. There wasn't a kiss, but her head fell against his chest. Her body went slack and suddenly, Slate was struggling to keep her on her feet.

He swung an unconscious Vivian into his arms and joined others walking down the stairwell.

The bastards had gotten to her. Sometime while she'd been out of his sight, someone had hypnotized her or done something to make her attack him.

God, he hoped she could remember who. It might be the only way he'd forgive himself for not keeping his promise to keep her safe.

"What time is it?"

Vivian awoke, searching for the microwave clock that should have shown the time in its bright green illumination in the kitchen. She sat straight up, unsure where she was or who had a heavy arm across her midsection.

"You okay?" a male voice asked. "Have another nightmare?"

It all came back to her in the blink of an eye. No amnesia. Along with no possessions, no money and no bad guy. This wasn't a nightmare. It was real life. It was her living the hand she'd been dealt.

"Yeah, I'm fine." She glanced around, recognizing

that they were in Slate's bedroom. "Shouldn't I be at the main house?"

"Heath's there. We came here because you were sick. It seemed the easiest way to get us both cleaned up."

An alarm clock across the room indicated it was around one in the morning. She felt like someone had beaten her up. And her mouth felt fuzzy with a hint of rubbing alcohol. "Do they know who set the fire at the apartment building?"

"You mean the hospital?"

She got out of bed with the intention of using her new toothbrush. She desperately needed some water and… *Oh, my gosh!* She needed clothes.

She stumbled to the bathroom and without turning on the light, found a towel to wrap around herself.

"Slate. I thought we—were we stuck in an elevator?"

"That's the last thing you remember?" He flipped on the light next to his bed.

There was blood on his pillow. She looked at his head, where a bandage was stained and leaking. He saw the direction of her eyes and touched his temple, then looked at his pillow.

"No reason to be upset. It didn't even need stitches."

"Who did that?"

His raised eyebrows gave her the answer. She had. And she couldn't remember any of it.

"Why are we naked?"

"*We're* not. You vomited a couple of times on the way home. The doctors said you probably would, but it still got all over us the last time. You really don't remember this?" He shifted the blanket aside, showing his sweatpants.

He looked around the bed, then over the side and pointed to the floor. "There's the T-shirt I had you in. You kept telling me you were burning in a fire."

"Nightmares?"

"Yeah."

"And you're sleeping with me because…?"

"You couldn't sleep without me. You coming back to bed?"

"I…I need…" She snatched up the large T-shirt and retreated into the bathroom.

After the time it took to take a shower—because something was making her hair a greasy mess—she expected Slate to be sawing logs in a dark room. But he wasn't. He was scrambling eggs in the kitchen.

"The doctors who looked you over said soft foods. Scrambled eggs are soft, right? You think you could eat?" He turned around, pan in hand, still stirring the eggs. He arched his eyebrows and grinned. "You look much, much better. I hope that's a good sign."

"Maybe. My teeth aren't furry and my hair isn't greasy anymore."

"Eggs?"

She put her hand over her stomach as it growled. "I think so. But if I stop eating, I'm sure it's no reflection on the cook."

"Well, that remains to be seen. But what self-respecting bachelor can't scramble an egg?"

He filled two plates already on the table. One place

had a bottle of water and another had a beer. She took the place with the water bottle.

"So what happened?"

"You were obviously drugged. We won't know with what until the labs come back. Doesn't really matter since we don't know who did it to you."

She put her hand to her head. "Fuzz. It's all just a big blur."

"Sort of like Allan Pinkston and half of the sleep-study vets who had altercations for no reason." He smiled, but it was stiff and forced.

The humor was lost on her and she didn't quite understand what all the veterans had to do with her.

"So do you think that somewhere during the day someone drugged me and told me to—oh, God, you said I hit you. What did I hit you with?" She wanted to run to him, to get a closer look under the bandage at his temple.

"An IV pole. That was after the elevator stopped when the fire alarm went off." He shrugged like it was no big deal.

"So we were stuck in an elevator. Was there an actual fire? Did anyone get hurt?"

"Yes, we were. Yes, on the fourth floor. Only scrapes and bruises during the evacuation. And yes, they caught two vets. One set the fire and one pulled the alarm on a different floor."

"Two more men from the sleep study?"

He shook his head and took another bite of eggs. "You aren't eating and you should drink. They said you'd be dehydrated." Another bite. "No. These two are regulars in the ER. They said someone wearing a mask asked them to help with a drill."

"They believed that?"

"They were sort of out of it." He finished his last bite and started on his beer. "High on the oxy they'd been given."

She nibbled when he pointed toward her plate again. "Did I ruin everything?"

"Hell, no. We've got a list." He grinned, then pointed his beer toward her. "A limited list of people who had access to you. Whatever knocked you off your feet had to be ingested."

"But I don't remember anything."

"Believe me, Vivian. The rangers have worked with less. Whoever messed with you today underestimated just how good we are."

"And how humble."

He winked, tipping his beer at her. "Damn straight."

Chapter Twenty-Eight

Vivian loved seeing Slate's face smiling. In the past few days, when that deep furrow appeared across his brow, it had been because of her. Smiling was good. Smiling was great.

Avoiding her attraction to him wasn't. It made her feel all squishy inside. He was probably right about trying to begin something under these circumstances. But he was just so darn loveable.

And good Lord, that grin!

"Can I ask you a question?" She turned sideways in her chair to face him directly.

"Sure."

"When am I supposed to make a big deal out of being attracted to you? When's the correct time?"

"What? Where did that come from?" He looked totally surprised until he did his adorable eyebrow thing.

"From the fact that you are just so darn cute when you smile and waggle your eyebrows like that."

"Well, I don't think this is the best time. There's no telling if those drugs are affecting you some way."

She didn't care. At all. It was almost a compulsive

need to be close to him. "I can write a note stating I'm of sound mind and drug free if you want me to."

"For what?"

"For now." She used her feet to push his chair away from the table and was quickly sitting across his lap.

There was just something about him. Something honest and refreshing and strong and safe. She wanted to discover everything and what made him who he was. So it made perfect sense to kiss him again.

And maybe again.

"Did I finally come up with a way for you to say yes?" she asked.

"Was I saying no?"

"Man alive. Each and every time we get close to releasing all this tension between us. There's a definite no from you."

She leaned in to kiss him and he leaned back. She shook a finger in front of his face, then pushed her body completely against his, holding him in place. He couldn't escape her lips connecting with his.

"Say yes," she pleaded against his lips.

Slate's chest began to rise and fall faster under her hands. "Bad, bad idea," he said before crushing his lips to hers.

The Texas Ranger in him might think kissing her was a bad idea, but the man hauling her hips to his left nothing but good sensations behind.

"If this is your idea of bad..." she whispered, leaving the rest to his imagination. "You are such a good kisser."

"You make me crazy," he said. His lips covered hers completely.

They stopped talking. He pushed her arms higher around his neck and stood, keeping her next to him with his hands under her butt as he moved them from the kitchen to his bedroom.

The bed was still disheveled from where they'd slept earlier.

"You're sure? This isn't a funny reaction to drugs or confusion or something like that?"

She nodded, afraid that answering him aloud would somehow make him misinterpret her reply. The luxurious kiss she gave him should be answer enough. She couldn't let him go this time. Just to be loved…even for a moment.

He laid her on the bed, tugging off her shirt as he did. He pulled his off quickly, then unbuttoned his jeans. He lowered himself on top of her, dipping his tongue into her mouth, then slipping across her chin and skimming… everything.

Frantic touching and hurried clothing removal got them completely skin to skin for the first time.

Heaven.

She tasted the salt on his skin, nipping the curve where his shoulder muscle met his neck. She tilted her head back, encouraging him to taste her more, sending additional shivers of anticipation down her spine.

He lightly scraped his teeth across her breast before settling into the hollow of her throat. He quickly replaced his lips with his fingertips, stroking the edge of her bra. Then he caught her mouth to his again, plunging his tongue inside. He captured her whimper as their hips pushed against each other, searching for more.

"There's no turning back."

"Ranger Thompson, are you going to kiss me or talk me to sleep?"

He didn't debate the situation after that.

Desire was evident from both of them. There wasn't any need to delay what they'd both wanted and needed. He shifted and was inside her, filling every bit of her with every bit of him.

There may be consequences in the morning, but at the moment, all she could think about was the undeniable satisfaction. And how soon they could do it all again.

THE NEXT MORNING, consequences arrived with the dawn and a clear head. Only a couple hours of sleep for Vivian and then she was sipping coffee, watching the sunrise when Heath began feeding the horses. She joined him, pitching in without a word.

She'd volunteered to help. Heath treated her with what seemed like a little more respect. In spite of the fact that it was her fault Slate's roommate was taking on extra duties. Heath managed to feed the horses and chickens without much more than a grunt. But it was a respectful couple of grunts from the man of few words. He walked with her back to his house and kicked the couch as he passed to wake Slate up.

"You coming to work or going to sleep in?" Heath asked before going to his room.

Slate looked blurry eyed at his watch. "I've only been asleep a couple of hours. I came out here earlier to keep watch."

Heath didn't laugh much, but he did all the way into his room. Slate had to laugh since he'd fallen asleep keeping that so-called watch.

"We've got a psychopath to catch today," Heath yelled through his closed door. "But you can go back to bed if you want."

Slate was already sitting on the couch, rubbing his eyes, then stretching his arms above his head. "You doing okay?" he asked Vivian. "Get some shut-eye without fire nightmares?"

"Yes. I woke up about the time you fell asleep. Let me get you some coffee."

"Nice. Heath feed the horses?"

"We just finished." She handed him a cup and stepped back.

She wanted to know Heath's story. It seemed like he had one. But right now, today, he was very correct.

They had a psychopath to catch.

Vivian was ready to leave. It didn't take long to put on jeans, a pullover sweater and a pair of tennis shoes. Showers stopped as she cleaned the kitchen and tried to remember what had happened last night. She'd remembered most of what had happened in the waiting room and elevator.

No one had told her anything or pushed her to remember. Slate had explained that after Allan Pinkston, he'd been advised against saying anything to her. Anything that might create a false memory. But why couldn't she remember all of the tests the EEG lab had done on her?

As soon as Slate was out of the bedroom, she was

ready to get started. He, on the other hand, was gathering his things and looking toward Heath's room.

"Why do you seem like you're waiting for backup?" she asked after several minutes. "I'm not being left behind. What if I remember something?"

He glanced at his phone again. "The guys are kind of worried you might hit them over the head with an IV pole."

"Oh. I hadn't considered that."

"Look." He gripped her shoulders. "You're not getting left behind, but we still don't know who's doing what. So we have to take precautions."

"That's understandable. I agree. I'll sit in the truck."

"I was thinking more like you'd sit in the office with Wade." He patted her arms, making her feel twelve.

"Okay, Wade can sit in the truck, too."

"Oh." He pointed a finger at her. "You're funny. Very funny."

"And serious. I might remember more if I'm at the hospital."

"Might. Might not. There's no guarantee you'll ever remember." Again, Slate didn't act too concerned. "We have units collecting all the remaining sleep-study patients. Even your brother's been put into a separate holding cell under surveillance."

She let his words sink in. It made sense. But he was keeping it almost too low-key. No one knew what the patients had been programmed to do if something went wrong. And no one knew what she'd been programmed to do.

Oh, God!

Last night, she'd made it back to the waiting area before she got sick. There was no telling what she might have done if a knife or gun had been available when she attacked Slate.

"I'm not going to hamper your investigation by doing something selfish and stupid. You don't have to worry about me."

Slate released a long sigh of relief, and right on cue, his phone rang. She heard Heath's phone buzzing and vibrating in his room.

"What's happened?"

"Let's get moving," Heath said, coming out of his bedroom. "Looks like you're going to the hospital. We all are."

Chapter Twenty-Nine

Vivian was left waiting in the truck at the front entrance of the hospital. The rangers were parked one after the other on the street. Police cars blocked the entrance and both roads coming to either side of the VA.

One of the sleep-study vets had walked into the hospital with his police escort. Shaking the policeman's hand, he'd overcome him, then taken his gun. Now he was in the admitting office, holding hostages.

The hospital was on lockdown and the rangers were assisting the OIG in any way they could. All the police escorts had been warned about the incident, so they hoped none of the other patients would react this way. But nothing was certain.

Everyone needed answers.

Especially her.

She wished she had a phone or even a notepad to gather her thoughts. There was nothing. Actually, she wished she had Slate to talk to. Or take a look at his smile and feel completely at ease.

But even on the ride over, he wouldn't talk about what had happened yesterday. He was more than serious about not forcing the issue. And since Heath had ridden with them from the ranch...there hadn't been any hand holding or a kiss goodbye.

She pushed those thoughts from her mind, admitting that it was very hard to do because their time together had been so exciting and a relief after the past few days.

She had questions and focused her mind on each conversation, each movement, each person who'd escorted her from one test to the next. No one had given her a pill. Not even an aspirin.

So what had happened to her after the MRI? Then she went to the fifth floor. What was there? Something that had made her hair oily. Another test to check her... brain waves. That was it, she'd had an EEG. Women. There were two women giving her a test.

One in a white lab coat and the other had...

She jumped out of the truck, locking it behind her. She needed to search for Slate or a police officer who could call him outside. One of those two women had drugged her. There was only one person who'd given her anything all day. Mineral water with a funny taste and that probably wasn't water at all.

Abby. The woman they'd met earlier in the week. She'd had a face mask hanging around her neck, disposable gloves on her hands. They'd even told her their names, asked her questions. How convenient.

And if it wasn't her? Well, then at least they'd narrowed the suspects down to two instead of more than a dozen.

"Excuse me, officer."

"You'll have to go back, ma'am."

"But I've got to get a message to one of the Texas Rangers. He'll be with the OIG."

The officer—or more like a security guard—wasn't going to help her. In fact, he was already ignoring her and concentrating on evacuating the emergency entrance.

Vivian knew enough about the hospital now to walk around to the employee entrance. There was a guard there, but she waited for him to help someone who'd stumbled and then she passed through the doors like a fish swimming upstream.

Each door she came to on that floor was locked. The elevators weren't running. Were the rangers spread out through the hospital?

Was there a chance that she'd find Slate at one of the doors? She really did have every intention of finding him. But she didn't exactly know how to get to the different floor levels of doors or where he'd be.

If she asked permission from one of the team, he would send her back to wait in the truck. Slate would probably escort her there himself. And if she told the others the truck was locked, he might turn her over to the police. She wouldn't put that action past any of them. By then, the EEG lab staff would probably be gone. So Vivian headed to the fifth floor.

Someone needed to stop the lab technicians responsible for all this chaos. She was available.

It was the perfect time to catch a psychopath.

THE SITUATION AT the VA Hospital was out of control. Totally out of control. And there wasn't a damn thing lowly Slate Thompson could do about it. By the time the rangers arrived, they were just more law enforcement officers under the direction of the hospital's OIG.

Investigating fraud or a physician's misconduct was completely different from a hostage situation. Very hard to explain that the rangers believed the veteran was under some kind of brainwashing. Or that the situation was a cover to get one or two people out of there without being caught.

The OIG couldn't contend with a possible scenario like that when they had a full-blown crisis actually happening. They had procedures that would be followed this time. And of course, if it did have something to do with the sleep study and the fire set by two veterans the previous day, deviating from protocol had caused those problems. So the OIG was definitely not interested in allowing any additional guesswork.

Then when the hostage negotiator arrived...the hospital received a bomb threat. Unverified of course. But instead of employees and patients remaining where they were, everyone had to be evacuated.

Each Company B ranger who made it to the hospital took a different door to watch. Their commander tried to help the OIG handle the building evacuation. His second in two consecutive days, and according to Major Clements, he was madder than an angry hornet and more stubborn than a two-headed mule.

Chaos had nothing on the mass exodus from this place. Slate kept checking his phone, looking at the pictures of the men and women who had seen Vivian the day before. The hospital had confirmed that three of them weren't on the schedule, but that didn't mean they couldn't be in the crowd.

There were staff members on their suspect list, and searching those exiting had made his eyes cross for a while. But now the ambulance entrance was almost empty. Easy work compared to keeping his thoughts off Vivian.

How was he going to protect her if...?

"Exactly why you shouldn't have slept with her, you idiot," he told himself.

A silver-haired man in a white coat passed him and smiled knowingly. Slate's statement had probably been made by lots of men. Before he had to explain, his phone rang.

"Tell me something good, Wade."

"I'll tell you that I just saw Vivian run through the employee entrance and toward the stairs."

"Dammit. What's she doing?"

"You know I can't leave my post, man."

"Thanks for the heads-up."

He didn't wait for permission, didn't check in with his commander. He ran through the building, checking for directions along the way.

VIVIAN WALKED THROUGH a panicked hospital, asking directions, looking at signs. She hadn't passed additional rangers or law enforcement. Just confused patients and employees. She finally got close to the stairwell that should take her to the fifth floor when she noticed a woman in a lab coat wearing a mask.

When Vivian caught up with her, it wasn't Abby or

Lucy. A sense of relief and disappointment swept over her as she entered another stairwell and continued walking to the fifth floor.

This set of stairs was the one a nurse had told her led directly to the wing where the EEG lab was located. It was a long process getting up the stairs while people were coming down. But the initial crowd had thinned.

Someone seemed to be running just below her, also heading up the stairs. She stopped a second later after she squeezed past a wheelchair wedged to hold the exit door open on the fourth floor.

She looked around for some way to defend herself and found nothing. She stepped behind a door that separated the elevators from the rest of the hall. The wheelchair stuck in the exit moved.

What would she do?

"Vivian?"

"Oh, God. Slate?" She ran out from her hiding place. "I can't believe you found me."

"Why aren't you in the truck?"

"It's the EEG lab. They gave me a bottle of mineral water. It could have been drugged. I remembered and I've been trying to find you. They wouldn't let me inside."

"Slow down, babe. They wouldn't let you inside because they've had a bomb threat."

"I thought it was a man with hostages."

He nodded. "What's this about the EEG lab?"

"It's either Lucy or Abby. You remember the woman who introduced herself in the cafeteria? My money's on her. She was curious about what we were doing and had one of those surgical masks tied around her neck. I saw it hanging around her neck both days."

He snapped his fingers. "The person who hired the veterans to pull the fire alarm wore a mask. Let me text their names to Heath."

"We need to go. Now. The women might still be in their office." She laced her fingers with his and started toward the stairwell. He didn't budge.

"I text first. Then we have backup on the way. Heath will call for background on both of the women." He squeezed her hand. "Don't worry. Both of them were already on our list. If they tried to leave, we would have seen them."

Slate's texting took longer than she thought it should. He was clicking his screen so slowly that she almost offered to type the message for him. But it was obvious he'd had some responses, maybe instructions.

When he put the phone in his back pocket, he took his badge out and clipped it to his chest. He also took his suit jacket off and removed his weapon from its holster.

"I hope they're not telling you to take me back to the truck or lock me in a broom closet."

"No closets. You're staying with me. It's the only way I can guarantee your safety. Afraid we're heading down to the first floor, though."

"Slate, please. You have to catch whoever's responsible for yesterday. For today. For all those men and women affected. Don't stop when you're so close. They're going to get away and—" She couldn't say that her bother would go to jail for murder.

They were so close.

And she was three steps ahead of him. She darted to the stairwell. He was right behind her, but at least he was still behind her. The stairs going up were clear, but he caught her just three steps from the fifth floor.

"Come on, Vivian. You know we can't go in there."

They were both breathing hard. She sank to the step, knowing he was right.

"I need...I need to rest."

He sat beside her. "Jack's checking it out. We'll know soon. But remember, we have to find evidence, babe. Without evidence we can't do anything."

"But I remember."

"You remember one of them handing you a water that could have been drugged by anyone with access to the lab. I'm not a lawyer, but that's a pretty big pool of people."

"I know it's the assistant. There's something off about her. She tries too hard."

He took her hand and stood. "Let's go." He led her back to the fourth floor to the two chairs in a waiting area near the elevator. "We'll stay here. But I swear, I'll cuff you if you run again."

"I won't. I promise."

His phone buzzed and she waited impatiently while he silently read first one message, then another and still another. She bit her tongue, waiting for him to tell her what was going on.

"Jack's called for an emergency unit. The lab tech is unconscious."

"The tech or the assistant? Medium height or short?"

"He's got his hands full."

"It's safe now, right?" She walked toward the door. "We can go see."

He seemed to ignore her, checking his phone again. But as soon as he put it away, he rattled his handcuffs and led the way to the staircase. "You are staying in the hall. No exceptions. None. I'll see if I can identify her and you aren't doing anything. Please don't make me regret this."

"Thank you."

In spite of the bomb threat, an emergency team stepped off the staff elevator for transporting patients. They ran down the hall while she and Slate skirted the wall. The closer they got to the EEG lab, the harder it was to move her feet.

"I can't…I can't go."

"It's okay. Stay here and I'll go check."

"But—"

It was no use. A part of her mind kept telling her she didn't have an appointment. Her mind kept silently screaming that she couldn't return to the EEG lab without an appointment. She knew it.

She wanted to reach out and force Slate to take her with him, but nothing worked. Not her feet or her mouth or even her hands. She latched onto the handrail running the length of the hallway and hoped she didn't fall down.

It was a strange sensation that she'd never experienced before. But somehow she knew she had.

"Hello, Vivian. I was hoping we'd meet up today." Abby Norman came out of an office across the hall.

"Remember, Vivian. You don't have an appointment. Come with me."

Help. She could only shout the word in her mind. She couldn't call for Slate or anyone else. Abby's face was covered, she was in a lab coat that had Lucy's name on it and she had a wheelchair.

"This is going to be fun, Miss Watts. Lots and lots of fun."

Chapter Thirty

Vivian was in a state of complete numbness. Abby put a face mask over Vivian's nose and mouth, a knitted hat over her hair, tilted her head to the side and draped a hospital blanket across her lap. She used the elevator to go downstairs. Once in the lobby, Abby was joined by a man in a lab coat, and he escorted them out the ambulance entrance.

The man took over pushing the wheelchair. Abby bounced down the ramp, across the sidewalk and down to the street. Abby showed her hospital badge to the police officer there and they continued across northbound Lancaster Road.

"I can take it from here, Roger. See you tomorrow. Hopefully we'll get to work all day."

"See ya tomorrow." He waved and crossed southbound Lancaster.

"See, Vivian," the awful woman whispered in her ear. "Nobody has any clue that I'm responsible for everything that's happened. I literally wheeled you out of the hospital and no one even knows."

Vivian wanted to cry out. Scream. Yell. Pull the

woman into the street and have a brawl that would gather a crowd. But she couldn't move.

Drugs or brainwashing or even a simple hypnotic suggestion…she didn't know which. She couldn't force herself to move.

Abby pushed her to the marked disabled entrance for the Rapid Transit. She was being so casual about everything. Her voice remained calm and in charge, but Vivian watched her adding a set of cloth white gloves to the disposable pair she already wore.

Speak, she commanded herself. Nothing happened behind the surgical mask.

Abby sat on a bench next to the wheelchair. "I can see you getting frustrated and upset. The more I try to understand the emotions everyone cares so much about, the more I'm glad they don't affect me. I hope you're smart enough to realize that I thought through my escape."

They were joined by two additional hospital workers, who waved at Abby as if they knew her. They weren't surprised Abby was there and if they were curious about her pushing a woman in a wheelchair, they kept the questions to themselves.

Vivian concentrated on lifting her hand, trying to reach out for the door or seconds later one of the poles within the train car. It worked until Abby saw her hand and moved it back to her lap.

"Stay there and obey." Two stops and Abby got them off the train. "I could leave you here, but I've been told you're my insurance policy. A guarantee that I get away.

Personally, I don't see why you're worth the effort. But the advice is from someone close to me so I'll follow it."

The Rapid Transit station was on a hill. Vivian was grateful someone advised keeping her alive since Abby could have pushed her down what amounted to two flights of stairs.

There would have been nothing she could do except fall.

Yes, she's missing. And yes, she left the truck earlier. But I'm telling you, sir, she didn't have a reason to leave." Slate had explained this to Major Clements, who had taken him at his word. It was the VA OIG who didn't believe him.

Slate was just outside the south side of the building in a command center. The hostage negotiator had successfully kept the sleep-study patient talking while SWAT stormed the office and took him into custody before he could kill himself.

Minutes were ticking off the clock that had begun the moment he'd stepped from the EEG lab. Lucy was dead of an overdose. They didn't know what had killed her, but the water bottle near her smelled of almonds so everyone assumed she'd been poisoned.

The building was being cleared floor by floor because of the bomb threat. Slate had unsuccessfully tried to get security to also look for Vivian. But his gut told him she wasn't there. She'd been certain Abby Norman was responsible. And now Abby's supervisor was dead.

Too much of a coincidence.

"Hey." Heath caught his attention.

"Did you get it?"

"She lives a couple of blocks from here. I'll text Jack and Wade where we're headed."

"No. Only one of us can afford to be fired. This is on me and me alone." Slate took his badge off and put it in his jacket pocket. "Text me the address."

"Don't do anything crazy, like get dead. Your mom will kill me."

"Give me fifteen before you tell the old man I'm gone."

"You got it."

The address came through and a couple of clicks later Slate was following the directions. Heath had been correct. Denley Drive ran parallel to Lancaster Road. He turned at the second intersection when the Rapid Transit train left the middle of the street.

He parked in front a gray house that was clearly built outside of the surrounding price range. Brand-new house on a block where the neighbors clearly didn't pay for garbage pickup. The end of the street just past the Rapid Transit lot was full of bags and loose trash.

Abby Norman's home was directly across from the Rapid Transit commuter parking. A person could drive straight from her driveway right into the lot. The yard was fenced off, surrounded by trees and groomed bushes. It had a detached garage but no sign of a dog. Which was good, since Slate had opened the gate to go to the front door and knock.

The suspect came to the door with a forced smile on her face.

"Miss Norman? I hope you remember me from the hospital cafeteria."

"Of course I do. You're the Texas Ranger who asked about Rashid. Did you discover why he went crazy like that? Did you need more information about his visits?"

"No, ma'am. That's not why I'm here."

"Oh?"

Her expressions had a well-rehearsed sense to them. He'd seen practiced sentences before, but this took it to a whole new level. Now that he was paying attention, he understood what Vivian had picked up on.

"May I come in?"

"Certainly. Do you mind if we have our discussion here in the foyer? I don't often have guests and don't have a formal room to entertain."

"I was wondering, Miss Norman, if you came to work today. There's been an incident."

"Oh, no. Not another murder."

"As a matter of fact, yes."

"After all the commotion yesterday, my patients—I mean the ones that come to the lab—were canceled. The hospital was fine with me staying home."

He stood, traditional hat in hand, trying to observe everything about the house. Looking for a possible struggle, listening for any signs of Vivian.

Nothing. He had no probable cause.

Nothing besides everything shouting at him that Vivian was here.

His phone vibrated inside his jacket. "Excuse me a second." He took it out and bent his head to read.

Slate didn't see what slammed into the side of his head. All he saw was a blur and had no time to duck.

Chapter Thirty-One

Vivian heard the casual conversation. Abby had invited someone with a deep voice—who sounded a lot like Slate—inside the house. Muffled words kept her from hearing what was said. Her present semidrugged state kept her from crying out. There was a crash and then a slam against the polished floor.

Oh, God. Oh, God. Oh, God. Was he unconscious or even...dead?

Vivian felt the bubble of panic forming in her chest. The cloth over her mouth helped keep her from hyperventilating. What wild imagination had ever convinced her she could find a murderer or help her brother? She should have stayed in the truck or better still, stayed at Slate's house.

Now she'd gotten him killed. He needed her help. Suddenly, the power of suggestion that she couldn't get up was gone. She was free. She could move. She felt sick, but she could move.

She ran to where she'd heard noises. It was Slate. Facedown on the floor, a silver tray and broken glass around his head. Abby was picking up the pieces and neatly stacking them in a trash can.

Vivian skidded to a halt as Abby grabbed one of the larger pieces and held it to Slate's neck. The madwoman pushed it just under his ear. It was sharp enough to draw a drop of blood.

"No! Don't...don't hurt him. I'll...I'll do whatever you want."

Abby handed her a small bottle of water like the drugged mineral water from the day before. She continued to pick up the glass and missed that Vivian poured most of the water onto Slate's pants leg. He had a huge knot on his head. She instinctively reached to help him, but Abby snapped to attention.

"She said we need to leave. We'll drive to the airport. I can change my ticket."

"Why are you doing this? What are you getting from killing all these people?"

"Remember, Vivian. You don't have an appointment. Do as I tell you."

Vivian sought Slate with her eyes but couldn't will her body to move toward him.

"My reasons are far above the intelligence in your average mind." Abby reached onto the credenza and pulled out a pair of disposable gloves, then handed them to Vivian. "Put these on. You can't contaminate my things with your germs."

Abby had done something to control her. A posthypnotic suggestion that was working.

"Remember, Vivian. You don't have an appointment. Come with me."

They left the house and slowly made their way across a new sidewalk. There seemed to be a certain place on each square that Abby had to walk. She didn't let anything touch her and the only thing Vivian had been handed was a single key to a car.

The garage door had a code, which Abby punched in. The door lifted to show some type of very expensive white sports car. Vivian was getting a little punchy. It was harder to focus than usual.

One piece of information kept repeating in her mind. *Do this and Slate is safe.* She pinched herself while getting into the car, trying to wake herself up.

"Good thing I'm not driving," she said, feeling kind of weird. Or drugged. She explained why automatically. "I can't drive stick."

Abby carefully put everything into the car. Vivian automatically latched her seat belt. Her abductor didn't for some reason, but Abby backed out of the building and the driveway anyway. She put the car in gear and took off.

It must have been fast because Vivian was pushed back in her seat for a second or two. "I need out of here." She tried to open the door, gaining more control of her mind. Pushing away the suggestion that she needed to obey.

Abby clicked the auto lock button.

"No. No. No." Vivian tried to reach across the other woman to unlock the doors. She tried to grab the steering wheel but her fingers slid. She stretched again, leaning against the other woman.

Abby screamed when she was touched, throwing up

her hands. She lost control of the sports car, which went flying off the road.

Vivian was stunned. Literally. The seat belt jerked her backward. The airbags went off. A cloud of white powder coated everything, hanging in the air.

Abby began screaming hysterically. And kept screaming. Vivian covered her ears, it was so disturbing and bad. Horrible.

Even in a slightly drugged or hypnotic state of mind, Vivian could tell the older woman seemed to be having some sort of mental break.

"I need to be perfect. This can't be happening. My research. Everything's ruined. I'm ruined. Get out!" She pulled a knife and cut Vivian's seat belt, then plunged it into the airbag screaming, "Out! Out!"

Grabbing hold of Vivian's hair, she dragged her across the console and out the driver's side door. She kept the knife on her, holding her close.

"We've got to get to the train. I need…I need…my perfect death."

SLATE COULD FEEL…and he could still see. He pushed himself up from the floor. Or sort of tugged himself upright using the credenza that he'd been lying beside.

Putting his hand to his head, his fingers came away bloody.

Vivian! Where had they gone?

He stumbled through the small, sterile house. No Vivian. No suspect. He took out his phone and called Wade while he stumbled out the front walk. There across the parking lot at the corner farthest from him were the two women. Abby Norman led Vivian away from the station.

Toward the oncoming train.

He started running.

"Get out of the way! Train! Let her go!"

Chapter Thirty-Two

"No, Ranger Thompson. I won't," Abby shouted. "No one will see this for what it is. I need the perfect death and none of you are going to stop me from obtaining it."

Abby Norman was strong for a woman of her slight build. That or she'd drugged Vivian again. Vivian didn't have a mad, glazed-eye look but she wasn't struggling. Maybe it was part of Norman's programming the day before.

He saw the wrecked car at the end of the road. Vivian seemed sort of stunned. Then he saw the knife at her throat.

But she wasn't fighting back. Why? Was she in a trance like before?

"Vivian, honey, how did you get free?" he asked loudly, not caring if Abby Norman heard him or not. "If you get the chance, get free. Remember how you got free from me. Wake up!"

The Rapid Transit train whistle blew. It was at the previous block, crossing the intersection. They didn't have much time.

"Vivian! Fight!"

Slate ran across the parking lot for the stairs leading up the hill to the train stop, keeping his eyes on the women. No one was at the stop so he couldn't call for help. No one was there to stop a madwoman from walking onto the tracks in front of the train.

The steep incline up to the train stop was reinforced with a concrete wall. He couldn't climb it so he had to follow the sidewalk from the parking lot. Up two sets of steps and around to the loading area before he could run onto the track and follow them.

He was on the first set of steps. The whistle was blowing nonstop. The brakes were screaming, trying to stop…

"What are you doing? Let go of me." Vivian was alert and finally fighting. She knocked the knife out of her opponent's hand but couldn't get her hair free.

Slate hit the top of the second set of steps and began running. The fastest way was straight down the track. He waved, he shouted.

And he watched as Vivian threw several punches that her captor couldn't recover from. Abby fell, still holding Vivian's long hair and bringing her down to the track, too.

"The train is coming!"

Screeching brakes. Earsplitting whistle. Car horns blared. People screamed.

Vivian was on her knees.

Abby had a perfect smile on her face.

Slate got to Vivian with seconds left, just as the former army soldier kicked out and freed herself.

He grabbed Vivian around her waist and fell out of

the train's path. It barely missed them. It didn't miss Abby Norman.

Lying on the track as she was, she died horrifically and instantly. The train slid to a stop. There was nothing the conductor could have done. People from across the street ran toward them. There was blood on the track under the train.

Slate dragged Vivian into his lap. She was crying and mumbling incoherently.

"It's okay. You're okay." He repeated the same words over and over again. While rocking her in his lap, he kept her face pressed into his chest, kept his hand over her eyes.

There was no reason for her to ever have a memory of what was in front of them. He'd keep the unpleasant scene in his head for legal reasons, but Vivian didn't need it.

She'd have enough nightmares based off of the actual event. The feel of having her abductor yanked from her hand, hit by the train. Hell, she was probably more equipped to handle the whole ordeal than he was. She'd been in the military. Had served overseas. No telling what she'd seen or had to do there.

But still… He could keep her from seeing this particular incident. No reason to force more into her mind.

Life had enough horror.

SLATE'S HEAD HAD A LUMP the size of Rhode Island on the side of it. Being hit with what felt like a brick wasn't pleasant, but he wasn't dead. The EMTs gave him a green light to be checked out by his own doctor. He might have stretched the truth a little about passing out.

So he'd be more truthful with his own doctor...but later.

He needed to get back to Vivian. He'd been keeping an eye on her, but she was sitting in the back of the major's SUV. At least the heater was running for her. Wade sat in the front but wasn't talking. He was actually texting Slate, who could only read and not respond.

She's fine. Doesn't want to talk about it. Wants to wait for you to give her statement. Would rather stay in the SUV until you're done.

Four texts, several minutes apart. If they'd moved her, Wade would have let him know.

"Sign here that you're refusing transport." The EMT stuck a clipboard and pen in front of Slate. "I really think you need stiches, Mr. Thompson. I'm taking a wild guess here, but I think you've got a concussion. So if you start vomiting or lose consciousness, find an ER, stat."

"Yeah. We good?"

The EMT shook his head but turned back to his vehicle. Slate hightailed it to the dark SUV.

"You can't be alone with her, Thompson. You know we have to take your statements independently," Major Clements said.

"I want her to have a lawyer."

"Good idea. So you think she needs one?" Jack asked.

"No. But it'll keep anyone questioning her in line. She shouldn't be alone."

"I'll call mine."

"Thanks. Now have Wade roll down the window." No, it wasn't a question asking for permission. It was a demand that he expected to be met.

The window went down without a word. Three rangers besides himself were listening to the conversation. Wade got out of the driver's seat and joined Major Clements, Jack and Heath in a semicircle that prevented anyone from interrupting them.

"I know what you're going to say," she said with very little emotion.

"You do?"

"This was all my fault. Abby would be alive if I'd just waited in the truck."

"I was going to say…" he pulled a twig from her hair "…they're going to ask you what happened. Be honest. Jack's calling his lawyer—"

"You think I need a lawyer?" she asked, panicked but still avoiding looking at him.

"No, I don't. I just don't want you to be alone." He wanted to open the door and pull her into his arms. He couldn't. Too many eyes were watching. "A lot of departments will be asking you the same questions. Don't get frustrated or hyperventilate. Having a lawyer there will help."

She should have reacted to his tease about hyperventilating. She didn't move, but the men around him did. Out of the corner of his eye, he saw their hands go up, heard his commander say, "Give him a second."

"I've got to go, Vivian. Jack will take care of you. All the guys will. I'll see you in a few hours."

She looked pale, unusually still as the window slid up between them.

"You sure you're both okay to face these guys?" Jack asked. "Maybe the hospital should be our first stop?"

"I think she's in shock. Any chance of getting the questions postponed?"

He shook his head. "You know this jockeying-for-position battle is out of my hands. I'm not leaving and will get her out of there as soon as I can." He nodded to a group of officers coming toward them. "You take care of business."

Chapter Thirty-Three

Done. Over. Another case for the files. And freaky as hell. Slate couldn't remember anything more weird or strange happening to people he knew.

Martha Abigail Norman Toliver had been a very sick individual. Major Clements and the VA OIG had notified her parents in Florida. He was curious to hear what they thought of their daughter.

Slate had changed and was at home when he called Wade for an update, knowing he'd be working his way through the punishment files so he could get off desk duty sooner. *His friend really needed a reason to leave the office.*

"Any word on the why?" Slate asked. "Clues to what motivated her?"

"The forensics team is still cataloguing items," Wade said. "This case is three jurisdictional-messed-up nightmares. Nobody knows who to report to so getting any information is crazy."

"But you went to the house. What was it like?" Slate had seen through the door. Everything was white, sterile. It almost looked vacuum sealed.

"Her parents verified that sessions with Dr. Roberts was part of their agreement with Abby to pay her bills. Dr. Roberts's office confirmed our mild-mannered lab assistant was a patient. She must have helped herself to the Subject Nineteen records. The circumstantial evidence against Victor was that he had an appointment with the victim. Then he confessed and everyone stopped looking further."

"That should clear Victor Watts. Vivian's going to want her brother out of jail pronto. How long do you think it'll take?"

"Days. But I don't think we'll have to wait long. But I got my doubts about sending him back on the streets."

"That's where I'm collecting on my favor, man. I did you one, now it's your turn."

"You got it."

"Take a look into Victor's attorney. I want to know if he's getting a kickback from the investigators he recommended to Vivian. She and her brother will need money to live on. And are there any places hiring where we can give them some recommendations?" Slate swallowed hard.

They'd known each other less than a week, but he didn't want Vivian to move back to Miami. A different city in Texas…he could handle that. Texas was a big state and rangers transferred companies from time to time. But breaking into another law enforcement agency in Florida…that was another story.

"You're using your favor on this? I thought you'd want something harder. Or the truth about Jack's girlfriend."

"This is important. It's going to be a fight to get her

brother into a facility that deprograms minds—if there is such a place. In fact, all of the veterans who were exposed to Abby Norman are going to need it."

"I know, man. I've got your back and theirs. I'll make sure it happens."

Slate pressed his lips together and nodded. "Vivian will need to be checked out, too."

"Get this, the parents told us she had OCD and several other phobias and disorders." Wade changed the subject. "And apparently, she had a psychotic break recently. No one confirmed schizophrenia, but it was suggested that's why she was being observed by Roberts."

"I don't envy the team having to look and sort through all that."

"Hey, before I let you go. Norman had several files on the laptop they found in the wrecked car. They seem to be different stages of her—for the lack of a better word—brainwashing files she played for the vets. Looks like she'd drug them and play the files while they slept."

"Hope that helps the doctors find a way to fix everybody." *Even Vivian.*

"Same here. Gotta run and I still owe you a favor."

They hung up just before she got out of the shower.

"Is it really over?" She laughed, shaking her hair free of its towel. "How soon do you think Victor will be free? Major Clements explained it would take a few days. I could go see him before that and tell him what happened. That deserves a visit, right?"

"I'll call County and arrange a time. I just spoke with Wade. It looks like there's corroborating evidence at Abby's house."

"I can't talk about this again." Her words had a frantic tone to them and didn't match the bright smile she displayed. Her actions were very casual, as if she were brushing everything off.

"You don't want an update?"

"Not anymore tonight. I'll leave the rest for the appropriate authorities to muddle through. Victor will be released and that's all that matters to me." She fluffed her curls, finger-combing as she tilted her head to one side. "Wipe the scowl off your face, Ranger Thompson. Do you have ice cream?"

"I don't think so, but we can run out for some if you want."

"Oh, wow. I just realized I haven't eaten since the scrambled eggs. I bet you haven't either. Did your mom leave any leftovers?" She popped off the couch and pulled open the fridge.

"Vivian!" His voice was louder than he'd planned.

"What? Do you want a hamburger instead?"

He held his arms open. She'd avoided him after the accidental death of Abby Norman. She'd pulled away from every pat on her shoulder offered by the team or by rescue workers. She'd avoided eye contact while speaking about it to each department head who asked her questions. And now she wanted to act like nothing had happened.

She shook her head. Her mouth opened and shut again, followed by flattened lips that looked determined not to say a word.

"You can't do this to yourself," he whispered. "Come here."

"I don't want comfort for what happened," she said finally.

The sky was darkening, causing the room to darken, as well. He waited while the light from the open refrigerator door illuminated this woman he'd come to admire so much.

"I've said this before, but you didn't ask for any of this to happen. You left everything behind to rush to the side of your brother. You've been going ninety-to-nothing with one goal and you accomplished it. Now it's time to take a moment. Come on."

He wiggled his fingers, taking a step toward her, but still not touching. He gave the fridge door a one-finger push and she let it close. He still had an open arm but used it to coax her to the living room.

Barefoot and in pj's, she grabbed the couch throw that had been used more in that week than the year it had been draped over the arm of the uncomfortable chair in the corner. She curled her long legs into the corner cushions, leaving room for him on the opposite end.

Slate shook his head, refusing to be separated from her again. They'd been through a lot together in the past several days. He hoped she'd be around for several more. But it all depended on how he handled the next few moments.

He moved to the end of the couch behind Vivian, removed the cushion to make more room and squeezed his body in behind hers. She didn't give an inch until the last second. They sat there with no words. There weren't many that would mean much.

Vivian had almost been killed, and the woman chasing her, the woman responsible for all her pain of the past year, had died trying to finish her.

"It's okay to let it out, babe. We all do."

"I don't feel anything except relief," she whispered.

"That's okay, too. You have permission to feel that way. You also have permission to be glad you're alive. To be glad the train didn't hit you."

"I killed someone."

The only reason he heard her speak was because there weren't any other sounds in the house. She'd been in the military; hadn't she seen death before? Should he tell her how proud he was of everything she'd done today?

He wrapped an arm around the top of her shoulders, resting on the front of her chest, keeping her close and protected. Her cool fingers clung onto his forearm. She held on, dropping her forehead to join her fingers.

He didn't do or say anything else. He wanted to but training kept him silent. Or maybe it was experience from the way his parents had treated him and his sister. Either way...he waited.

Silent tears graced his arm. Then sobbing shook the woman clinging to him. He rubbed her back, offering what he could. But this seemed like one of those times it was better not to say anything.

"I was in the war. I've fired my weapon but I've never seen someone die like that. Maybe I should feel justified or vindicated. Look at what she did. She was horrible. All those deaths."

"You've been through a lot, Vivian. Give yourself time to take it all in, time to heal."

"But why?" She took a deep breath. "I don't understand how someone could do the things she did."

"We probably never will. Her mind wasn't all there. Some things just can't be explained."

"So many died. It's so sad."

She cried a bit more, and soon the sobs were just long, drawn, shaking breaths. She turned, lying on his chest, keeping his arm around her. He thought she'd fallen asleep.

Maybe he was the one who drifted asleep since he startled awake at her words.

"Pardon?"

"I don't know what to do now," she whispered a second time.

"You keep going. We keep going. And don't be afraid to ask for help if you feel you can't." He was proud of himself. He wasn't being a jerk. Wasn't being a typical man. This was his sensitive side.

Because the only thing he really wanted to do now was finish what they'd each started. After all, she was a beautiful, attractive woman who he wanted to stay around. He could think of something other than sex.

"You know you can stay here, Vivian. If you feel comfortable, that is. There's the extra room at the house and Mom could always use some help until you're back on your feet. It wouldn't be charity since you'd be earning your way."

"Your dad already called and offered me the spare room. I'm still not sure that's a great idea. And when Victor gets out, that's two of us. We can't do that to your family."

"Um… Wade's doing some research. We think that all the sleep-study patients will need some intense therapy. He's looking for a place to handle that. He's good at sweet-talking people to make things happen."

She turned her face and parted her lips but shook her head instead of stating any disappointment she may have felt. She rested on him again. "Maybe I should join them?"

"You need to be checked out for sure. But you weren't exposed the same. You're not getting any crazy feelings to bonk me over the head again. Are you?"

"I don't know. There aren't any spare IV poles hanging around." She laughed. "I can't thank you enough for the kindness you and your family have shown to me. I'm grateful. And especially to all you guys at Company B. You not only saved my life, but you've also saved my brother."

There it was again, the desire to kiss the luscious lips that tilted in a smile. So close to his. He wanted her like a desperate man, but the timing was all off. So he sucked it up and behaved.

Even if they would let down their guards.

And yeah, even if Heath was staying in the main house to give them privacy.

And sure, her fingers were drawing little circles and had unbuttoned the top button of his shirt.

Dammit, he needed to behave…didn't he?

It was hell being a man and not knowing when the moment was right. She was better now. Did she need him as much as he needed her?

There was one way—okay more than one—to find

out. But kissing her and discovering what she'd do afterward was the solution he chose.

Vivian's ever-changing eyes looked up into his again and he bent his head to capture her lips. She twisted around and kissed him back. Her arms went around his neck and across his shoulders.

Definitely an answer when she didn't pull back, didn't stop kissing. Her arms brought him to more of a sitting position, then she straddled his lap. And yet he found himself questioning if this was the best thing for her or for them.

Yeah, that was a head-scratcher. What red-blooded American male questioned if the timing for sex was right or not?

He cupped her shoulders, lifting her away from him. Their lips held onto each other until the last possible micron.

"Is something wrong? Should we move to the bedroom?" She managed to get off the couch before he could actually form a question.

Maybe he was having second—or even third—thoughts about asking the damn thing. He had his hand in hers and had followed her halfway around the end of the couch before...

"I'm going to hate myself, but are you sure this is a good idea?"

"What? Going to your bedroom? Do you need to put something on the door to keep your roommate out?" She began walking again.

Slate stopped and twirled her into his arms. He used one hand to keep her there and the other to tilt her face to his. Standing closer to the window and the porch-light, he could see the redness in her silver eyes from crying. He used his thumb to remove a smudge from the corner of her eye.

"Are you sure this is what you want? Now? Tonight?" he asked softly.

"You know I can get free from this hold."

"Please don't head butt me," he teased. Then he affectionately kissed the tip of her nose.

"Yes, Slate. I'm sure. I wouldn't have kissed you now or before for that matter."

"I just don't want you to feel pressured."

"Oh, please." She raised her hands and cupped his cheeks. "Do not insult my integrity or intentions again."

His hands went in the air in an act of surrender. "Whoa, believe me, I am not accidentally going down that road a second time."

She brought his mouth to hers in a beautiful, sexy-as-hell kiss before sliding her hand up his arm to take his hand. She led him down the short hallway.

"Then come down this one with me."

Epilogue

Two weeks later

"Relax. You're taking this ride way too seriously." Slate meant it. If she didn't loosen up in the saddle, she'd be sore all over.

"I've never been on a horse before." Vivian continued to sit stiff and straight. "At least not out of the paddock."

"You're doing great. I still don't understand why you won't let me give you lessons."

"Because we'd end up not having a lesson. I'm working them off, you know. Learning how to groom and clean the stalls. And in exchange, your sister gives me a beginner riding lesson. She's pretty good."

"I could do that. Teach you."

"We tried. Our one and only lesson ended up in the hayloft."

"Oh. I didn't think you were serious back then. Besides, it was going to rain." He remembered that afternoon. It was the last time he'd kissed her, stopping just shy of… "In fact, it rained all afternoon. I'm just saying, I could give you lessons now. I've got more time."

He slipped off his mare and was below her in a couple of strides, lifting her out of the saddle. She put her hands on his shoulders and slid down his chest.

Her cheeks were red from the winter wind. He'd already switched the ball cap from blocking the sun, turning it backward on his head. The thick jacket he'd started off in was draped over the back of his saddle. He hoped it was the sun heating his body and not nerves.

"Aren't you cold?" she asked.

"Sunshine and love are warming me inside and out."

"As your father would say, you're being downright silly." Vivian drew her jacket a little tighter, emphasizing that he should be cool. "I'm still not moving into your room. Or did you bring me out here to tell me it was time to get my own place?"

"Of course not. You know you're welcome as long as you want to stay. Besides, I kind of like having someone take my turn in the barn."

"So you brought me all the way out here to the edge of the property, Mr. Thompson. Do you have a specific reason?"

"First, I thought taking a ride today would be nice. It's the first day I haven't worked since you moved in. We haven't been alone since."

"Since the hayloft."

Vivian dug the toe of her used boots into the dirt. She'd barely been making eye contact with him recently. She lived in his old bedroom at the main house and he'd rarely been home. She was helping around the ranch and looking for a permanent business position in Dallas to be near her brother.

When everything was straightened out at the VA

Hospital, another case had immediately required his full attention. He dived into work, trying to make up for all the ruckus raised by every official from here to D.C.

"And second?" she asked, wrapping the reins around her hand.

"It's the only way you'd agree to see me alone."

"True."

"Why? Did I do something?"

"You mean besides saving my life more than once, helping me free my brother, giving me a place to live? Oh, and let's not forget arranging for my brother to go to a hospital to make sure he wasn't still programmed by that horrible woman? And my treatment. Or maybe having Wade put in a few recommendations for my possible employment. Those things?"

"You know I meant did I do something wrong, Vivian." Slate took off his cap and scratched his head. He honestly didn't know what was going on. "I thought you liked me, sort of like we had a connection from that first glass of tea."

"We both got busy." She licked her lips. "And I do like you."

He unwrapped her mare's reins, which were now twisted in her hands, and looped them along with his around a low mesquite tree limb. He was sure the horses wouldn't run off. Not so sure about the filly standing in front of him.

Now that she didn't have the reins, he swept her hands into his and nudged her a bit closer. The fresh scent of her was on the breeze as vivid to him as rain on the horizon. He knew her...wanted her.

But he wasn't about to rush and mess things up the way he had when they'd first met.

"So I like you and you just admitted to liking me. Want to see a movie?"

"You're asking me on a date? Any chance you'd include dinner at a certain steak restaurant downtown?"

"Sure, I can arrange that."

"There's one more thing." She gently tugged her hands free and slipped them against his chest, then up around his neck. She tilted her head to the side slightly, looking at him invitingly.

He took her lips against his, tenderly at first, then more hungrily.

"What's your one more thing?" he asked against her lips.

"I'll need a good-night kiss."

"Oh, I can definitely see to that."

* * * * *

Look for the next book in USA TODAY *bestselling author Angi Morgan's*
TEXAS BROTHERS OF COMPANY B *miniseries,*
RANGER GUARDIAN, later this year.

And don't miss the first title in the series:

RANGER PROTECTOR

Available now from Harlequin Intrigue!

Get 2 Free Books,
Plus 2 Free Gifts—
just for trying the Reader Service!

 HARLEQUIN
INTRIGUE

SPECIAL EXCERPT FROM

HQN™

Lawson Granger thought he put his past behind him... until his first love, Eve Cooper, returns to Wrangler's Creek, Texas, with a baby on the way and a teenage daughter with questions about her real father...

*Enjoy a sneak peek of TEXAS-SIZED TROUBLE, part of the **A WRANGLER'S CREEK NOVEL** series by USA TODAY bestselling author Delores Fossen.*

She was dying. Eve was sure of it.

The pain was knifing through her, and the contractions were so powerful that it felt as if King Kong were squeezing her belly with his hairy fist. Her breathing was too fast. Her heart racing.

And now she was hallucinating.

Either that or Lawson Granger had indeed slipped in the puddle where her water had broken and was now dying from a head injury. Great. If it wasn't a hallucination, it meant she'd returned to Wrangler's Creek after all these years only to cause the death of her old flame.

Her old flame grunted, cursed and maneuvered himself onto all fours. So, not dead, just perhaps with critical internal injuries. Of course, anything she was thinking or considering right now could be blown out of proportion because of the god-awful pain that was vising her stomach.

"My water broke," she managed to say. "And my phone." She'd dropped it when one of the contractions had hit, and the phone was now scattered all over the stone entryway and hardwood floor.

Eve wouldn't mention that the reason her water had broken right by the door was because she'd been trying to hear who was talking outside the guesthouse. She'd thought it was another of her *fans*. Apparently not though.

"This is too soon," she muttered. "I'm not due for three and a half weeks. A baby shouldn't come this soon, should it?" Eve knew she sounded frantic, perhaps even crazy, but she couldn't make herself stop babbling. "Please tell me the baby will be all right."

Lawson lifted his head, making eye contact with her. Yes, he possibly did have a head injury because he looked dazed.

Oh, God. There was blood.

It was on his head and on the butt of his jeans. Eve saw it while he was still on all fours and trying to get to his feet.

"You're hurt," she said, but it was garbled because another contraction hit her. For this one, King Kong had brought one of his friends to help him squeeze her belly. Because Eve had no choice; she dropped to the floor.

She was sinking onto her knees just as Lawson was getting to his. He caught on to the wall and, grunting and making sounds of pain, he got to his feet. He glanced around as if trying to get his bearings, and he growled out more of that profanity. Some of it had her name in the mix. It definitely wasn't the sweet tone he'd used when they were teenagers and he'd charmed her out of her underpants.

Where will this unexpected reunion lead?
Find out in TEXAS-SIZED TROUBLE by
USA TODAY *bestselling author Delores Fossen, available now.*

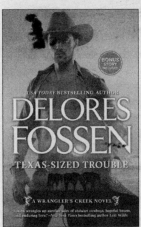

Need an adrenaline rush from nail-biting tales
(and irresistible males)?

Check out **Harlequin® Intrigue®**
and **Harlequin® Romantic Suspense** books!

New books available every month!

CONNECT WITH US AT:

Harlequin.com/Community

H HARLEQUIN®
™

**ROMANCE WHEN
YOU NEED IT**

SGENRE2017